DIRTY LITTLE CONVICT

SINNERS WELCOME

SAMANTHA BARRETT

To all my bad bitches that want to finger fuck their pussies in front of strangers but are too shy to do it.

I hope this book gives you the courage to embrace your inner sex demon and let that filthy little slut out to play...

Don't expect to go up north when your time comes because you'll be coming down south with me like a good girl.

To all my bad bitches that want to finger fuck their pussies in front of strangers but are too shy to do it.

I hope this book gives you the courage to embrace your inner sex demon and let that filthy little slut out to play...

Don't expect to go up north when your time comes because you'll be coming down south with me like a good girl.

ONE

LENNON

Two truths and a lie.

I told the lie but I never spoke the truth, and now I am being forced to live an empty life and live in envy of my best friend and her three boyfriends.

I had love once.

It was forbidden and so fucking wrong, but being wrong never felt so fucking good!

Kincaid Thatcher. The most forbidden fruit of them all, my stepfather.

Stone Thatcher. My wet fucking dream of a step-brother and my dirty little secret.

My mother sent the wrong Thatcher to prison. If only she could see me now. My tripod is set up at the end of my bed. I'm standing here in a skimpy pink bralette, pink crotchless panties, neon fishnet stockings and knee-high white come-fuck-me boots. My hair is teased and my makeup is thick. I made sure my smoky eye was on point so it would make the color of my green eyes pop.

I've had no choice but to rely on OnlyFans to fund my way through college. Mom cut me off the second she sent my stepfather to prison. She never loved Kincaid, she treated him like a second class citizen and spent the three years they were married opening her legs to everyone but him. I knew the only reason he stayed with that bitch was because of me.

I have guys that request private shows and ask me to do weird shit, I've turned them all down except for the three guys I get to put on a show for tonight. I have my three favorites that have requested a private show from me tonight, the three of them love to watch together. It sends a thrill through me that they never want me without the others being present, ever since Molly got her three guys, all I have dreamed about is having three of my own.

I've never seen their faces, never heard their real voices and that fact is what gets me off. Making myself come in front of the camera while three strangers watch is fucking euphoric and if you haven't tried it, you are missing the fuck out. I perch on the end of the bed, my legs wide open giving them a perfect view of my glistening pussy.

"You filthy whore, you're fucking drenched," *DaddyD* says—I only know them by their usernames.

I trail a finger through my folds and moan. "It's all for you, baby," I purr as I swirl my finger around my clit, arching my back.

"Finger fuck that dirty cunt, bitch," *HuxTheBux* growls. I push a single finger inside my tight wet little pussy and cry out. I don't do slow and sensual, I like it hard and fucking rough. I'm the type of bitch that likes my hair being yanked and neck choked until I nearly black out. All you can hear are the sounds of my moans and the squelching of my wet pussy as I drive my finger inside myself harder with each thrust.

"Oh, fuck," I pant.

"You want to replace that finger with our cocks, don't you, slut?" *RockHard* growls. I hate the sound of those stupid robotic voice distorters and want to hear him growl those filthy words in my ear. I love being called a slut and degraded, that shit is hot. I know some girls don't get into it, but I sure as fuck do.

I insert a second finger and cry out before I answer. "Yes, I want all three of your cocks inside each of my holes. I want to fuck you so bad." I'm breathless and panting, unlike other females, I can come from penetration alone and it's a fucking gift I was blessed with by the man above.

"Show us how fucking much you want our cocks

then, you dirty cunt," DaddyD barks. I tear the cup of my bra down with my free hand and squeeze my nipple. That small amount of pain sends me hurtling over the fucking edge. I scream out as my orgasm rips through me without an ounce of mercy.

The aftershocks haven't even finished coursing through me before HuxTheBux says, "Stay wet for us, slut, because we will be seeing you soon..." I don't even get a chance to register his words before they end the call. I stare at the camera in shock. Normally they stay until I have sucked the cum from my fingers and told them how sweet I taste.

I try not to let their dismissal bother me as I head for the bathroom and clean up. My pussy is needy and I feel unsatisfied, making yourself come is easy but it never feels as good as having someone else's fingers or cock inside you. Without warning, flashes of Stone naked and thrusting into me play like a reel. I try to shove those thoughts away but then they switch to me on my knees in the living room with Kincaid's cock rammed down my throat.

"Stop it!" I hiss to myself and force my mind to go blank, I hate reliving that memory. I never should have touched my stepfather. If I had just listened to him and stayed away he would never have been sent to prison. Kincaid and Stone could find me anywhere. I'm fucking terrified of the day that my past finally catches up to me and bites me in the ass.

I got away free while they paid for a crime they never committed, because I was too much of a coward to stand up and speak my truth.

Now I live with regrets every single fucking day.

A sigh escapes me as I check the time, then panic surges inside me. "I'm fucking late!" I screech, then begin dashing around my room to try to find something to wear. Tonight is the grand opening for Justin, Kingston and Brayden's new section of their club and I promised Lollie I would be there for her.

I rummage through my wardrobe and find the first nice mini dress I can get my hands on, then yank it off the hanger. It's white and will match my pink undergarments, thankfully, because I have no time to change them or even do my hair. I snag my phone and purse, then dash out the door.

I manage to order a Lyft as I make my way downstairs. I stand on the sidewalk, tapping my foot, hating that I'm going to be late so I type out a message to Lollie.

Me - I'm so sorry, babe. Running ten mins late 🥺

Her reply comes almost instantly.

Lollie - You promised!

Me - I know, babe. Work ran over and I lost track of time…

Me - Don't hate me 🙏

Lollie - 💀

Lollie - I could never hate you!

Lollie - Just hurry up and get here please

Me - My ride just arrived, be there soon 😇

I shove my phone in my purse as my Lyft comes to a stop at the curb. I climb in the back and release a loud exhale. If I could have gotten out of going tonight I would have. I love Molly and I'm so happy for her finding her guys, but I won't lie and say it's not hard to look at them all so loved up, knowing I will never experience that type of love again.

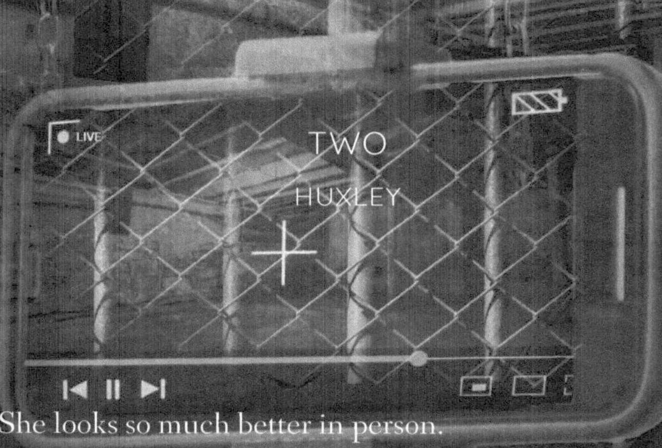

She looks so much better in person.

Lennon St James has no fucking idea how damn sexy she is without needing to try. The woman oozes sex appeal like no other, just the sight of her sitting in my back seat, gazing out the window, has my cock rock fucking hard. My mouth waters as I spy her fishnets and come-fuck-me-boots—the dirty little bitch didn't change after her video performance with us. The best part about it being dark out is the fact she can't see me checking her out.

The memory of how her pussy looked earlier slams into me and I have to bite down on my lip to keep from letting my groan slip free. As we near our destination, I grip the steering wheel tighter, she has no idea I'm about to fuck her life up for good tonight. She sits up straight as I pass the club and head around the back.

Her lips pinch to the side but when I bring the car to a stop at the back of the building, she begins to relax.

She reaches for the handle to get out but the door doesn't open. "What the fuck, dude?" she hisses.

"Sorry, forgot to take that off." I climb out of the car trying not to smirk, car child locks were the best invention. I pull the door open but keep my head down as she climbs out. Before she can make it two steps, I pull the rag from my back pocket, then dart forward and grab her from the back. She screams but I cut it off when I place the rag over her mouth and hold her against me. "Relax, convict, Daddy is waiting for you," I say a second before she passes out in my arms. I look around the empty lot to make sure no one is watching.

I lift Lennon into my arms and dart across the parking lot to the Cadillac idling in the back. My boy jumps out and pulls the back door open for me. I lay her on the back seat, then slam the door shut and climb in beside him. I just manage to pull my door closed as he slams his foot on the gas and peels out of there like the fucking po-po is hot on our tail.

"Did she see your face?" he asks.

"Nah, I made sure of that," I answer.

"Good, now grab the bag on the ground, there's a sedative in it. It should keep her passed out for the long drive." I follow his instructions then reach around the seat and jab the tip of the syringe into the side of her creamy thigh. A small whimper escapes her but she doesn't wake. I replace the cap on the tip then put it back in the small pouch.

"We really aren't gonna tell her anything?"

He shakes his head. "That girl's pussy is like a black hole, it sucks you the fuck in and never lets you go."

I snort out a laugh. "Her pussy looks nothing like a black hole, my friend."

"Fuck off, Hux."

I reach over and place my hand on his thigh. "She's the reason why you can never say those three words, isn't she?"

He releases a loud exhale and white knuckles the steering wheel. "That girl ripped my life apart and sent my dad to prison. She never told the fucking truth." Anger laces each of his words and I don't blame him. I love Stone but somewhere along the way between these video calls with her on OnlyFans, I've started to want her as much as *they* do.

"But you still want her, don't you?" He glances at me, his eyes tell me what his mouth won't.

He's still into his stepsister.

"Dad wants her bound and caged. As soon as we get to the cabin, take her to the basement. She isn't to know who the fuck we are and the masks will make sure of that. That little slut gets off on fear, the more scared she is the wetter her tight little cunt gets."

We pull up near the back of the cabin. Stone cuts the engine but neither of us attempt to get out of the car. I turn toward him and take in how tense he is, his face is contorted and I can see he is lost in his head. I reach out and cup his cock through his jeans, he hisses through his teeth and lolls his head to the side to lock eyes with me.

"Need me to take the edge off?" I offer.

He reaches out, grips the back of my neck and pulls me forward until his lips are on mine. The second his tongue tangles with mine I lose track of everything, nothing else matters but me and him. I start stroking him through his jeans, loving the sound of the groans escaping him. I try to deepen the kiss but the bitch in the back begins to stir, shattering our moment.

Stone pulls back and sighs. "Let's get her locked up, then I want you on your fucking knees in my room." He snaps his arm out and grips my throat. "You're going to suck my cock until I come down that pretty little throat. Only then will I allow you to fuck me. Am I fucking clear?" I love it when he gets rough and dominant with me.

"Yes, Sir." I dart my tongue out and lick my bottom lip, just to drive his ass crazy. His eyes narrow as his upper lip draws back in a snarl, making me laugh. "Let's go, I need to be balls deep inside that ass in the next twenty minutes or *I'll* make you suck my cock in the living room in front of your dad."

His eyes darken with lust. Stone likes getting freaky and trying new shit and is down for anything. Truth is, I want his dad to watch me as I fuck his son's face but Kincaid Thatcher isn't into dick, just pussy.

Well, more specifically *her* pussy.

We climb out of the car. Stone gathers her in his arms and I don't miss the way he peers down at her with equal parts longing and hatred. What she did to him and Kincaid is something that can never be forgotten, but I know as well as the both of them that this girl is one in a million. She would fit our weird-ass fucking trio and being able to fuck her whenever I want would be the cherry on top.

Nah, scratch that. Her watching me fuck her first love while she is chained up in the cage in the basement would be the best form of revenge.

The problem with Lennon St James is that she remembers Stone and Kincaid and how she fucked them over, but she forgot all about me the moment she sent Kin to prison for something he didn't fucking do all because her mommy made her do it! Everyone knows Karen was a bitch, she only wanted to marry Kincaid for his money. Stone told me she only fucked his dad once and that was it. If you ask me, I think Kincaid married that cunt so he could keep her daughter close because she is the real fucking prize after all.

My mouth feels like it's full of cotton balls, my body is aching and my head is pounding. How much did I drink at the club with Molly? I try to think back to what we drank but come up blank.

I didn't make it to the fucking club!

Memories of my Lyft driver grabbing me and placing something over my mouth flashes through my mind. A whimper of fear escapes me and I hate that my stupid whore of a pussy is pulsating because of how terrified I am. I force my eyes open, instantly slamming them closed again when the bright LED light overhead burns them. I slowly blink them open. I try to move but my hands are handcuffed above my head, my feet are chained to the bottom of the... cage!

I'm in a fucking cage!

I tamper my panic down and try to remain calm,

but that all flies out the window when I look down and see my dress has been removed and I'm left in nothing but my crotchless panties, bralette and stockings. My boots are nowhere to be seen and my terror amps up to new levels.

"Help!" I scream, then instantly regret it when I begin to cough. My mouth is drier than my mom's snatch right now. I try to pull against the cuffs. I know it's useless and I can't break them, but I also refuse to just hang here and wait for that fucker to come down here and do God only knows what to me!

When the metal bites into the soft flesh of my skin, I growl in frustration.

"I'm gonna kill you!" I scream out. Not a minute later the room is plunged into darkness. A cold shiver slides down my spine. I get the sensation I'm being watched but not just by one person. My skin starts to crawl and I try to fight back the arousal coursing through me. The last thing I want is for that mother-fucker to come in this cage and feel how drenched I am thinking it's for *him*.

A gasp escapes me when a light flickers on, but it's a red light, only offering me enough of a glow to see...

"You've got to be fucking shitting me," I breathe out at the sight of three masked men standing there. Unlike Molly's masked stalkers, mine don't wear suits or sweats, nope. These fuckers are wearing long-sleeve flannel shirts, dark-wash jeans and combat boots. I would think they were identical except for the fact that the color of their LED masks are the same color as their shirts.

Purple.

Orange.

Red.

I try to think of a threat or something to throw them off, but then the purple one on the end steps forward and I jerk harder against my restraints at the sight of the fucking axe in his hand.

"Tick tock, little convict." His voice is distorted and sounds robotic.

"What the fuck does that mean?" I hiss.

Red and Orange move to flank Purple on either side. One of them holds a metal baseball bat and the other holds a... knife. What the fuck have I gotten myself into?

"Those shackles are set on a timer," Orange says robotically.

"In precisely three minutes, you will be free and that cage door will open," Red adds. There is something about red that has me on edge, he's bigger than the other two and somehow more intimidating.

I dart my tongue out to moisten my chapped lips. "What happens when I'm free?" I utter. The three of them release dark chuckles, which only serves to heighten my fear.

"Little convict, *little convict*, oh how I have missed you." I recoil from his daunting words. "We're going to play a game of hide and seek," Purple says.

I shake my head. "I don't want to play, asshole," I grit out.

Orange continues on like I never spoke. "You get to hide and we get to seek the prize."

"What the fuck is the prize?" I snarl.

"That dripping cunt. When we catch you, and make no fucking mistake, we... Will... Keep... You, you will take whatever the fuck we give you. None of this is about your pleasure, this is about us and our need for vengeance." Any retort I had on my tongue withers away at red's promise. "Tick tock, little convict." The lights shut off and I'm plunged into darkness. I begin to tremble when I hear the axe dragging along the concrete floor.

The silence is deafening and holds an eerie edge. I hate myself for being so aroused. It's a fucking defect of mine, getting off on fear. Time doesn't seem to stand still like I had hoped it would. In what feels like seconds my restraints release me and the door to the cage unlocks. Dread pools inside me.

What if I just stay in here?

I push that thought away when I remember how

each of them held a weapon, that makes the decision easy for me. It's so dark in here I can't even see my hand in front of my face. I blindly feel along the bars on the side until I reach the front of the cage. My arms are screaming with relief but pins and needles ripple through my limbs and anger courses inside me. How dare these motherfuckers kidnap me and lock me in a cage like some fucking felon!

I wince at the thought and push all thoughts of Kincaid from my mind.

I finally reach the door and slowly push it open, the hairs on the back of my neck are standing on end as I step a foot out of the metal doghouse. I wait for one of them to pounce on me, but nothing happens. I shuffle my feet along the ground and wave my arms around in front of me, feeling for anything. I almost weep when I feel a wall and then a door handle. All I need to do is find an exit, then I can make a run for it.

The fact I didn't show up at the club means Molly will have to know something happened to me and alert the police.

I gingerly pull the door open and pop my head out first. My brows furrow. No lights are on inside the house, but the moonlight shining through the large windows affords me enough light to see. I slink out and quietly close the door behind me. I shiver from the cold but ignore it as I tiptoe through the small home, trying not to make a sound. Tears prick the backs of my eyes when I make it into the tiny kitchen and spy a door. I move around the butchers block and force myself not to run, just keeping my steady pace in case they hear my loud footfalls. Just as I'm mere feet from the door, I reach out to grab the handle.

"Time's up, little convict." I scream in fright and whirl around until my lower back slams into the edge of the counter. The guy with the purple mask stands there with that fucking axe in his hand. I look around me and spot a knife block. I dart to my right and grab the largest one before turning back to my captor. His dark laughter has me trembling as I point the knife at him. "Breaking you is going to be the most fun I've had in years."

"Bring it on, you Jason wannabe," I spit, then turn and grab the door handle.

She tries to yank the door open but it doesn't budge. I remain where I am, leaving her to it because there is no escape for her from this place. This is her new fucking home until we say otherwise. For the foreseeable future she is our pet and we'll do whatever the fuck we like to her.

"Fuck!" she shrieks, then whirls around to face me with that knife held out in front of her. I spy Huxley from the corner of my eye entering the room, blocking her last escape. "I'll fucking kill you," she vows.

"You're pathetic," I grit out.

Her eyes dart around the small room, trying to work out an escape plan but it's futile, she'll never get past us.

"I'll make you a deal. Drop the fucking knife and I promise to let you come once tonight," Hux vows.

"I'm not fucking you!" she hisses.

Both Huxley and I chuckle. "No. *We'll* be fucking *you*, little convict," I say. Her eyes widen in surprise. I see the indecision plastered all over her face. "Either way, you aren't leaving this place and we'll still get what we want from you."

She nibbles her bottom lip and shakes her head. "Get fucked," she screams as she runs toward me with the knife in the air, ready to plunge it into my chest. I shift out of the way and grip her wrist in one hand, then whirl around so her back is plastered to my chest. I apply enough pressure to her wrist to make her cry out. She drops the blade and it clanks to the tile floor with a *tink*. "Please..."

"Are you begging, little convict?" I murmur in her ear.

She trembles in my hold. Hux pushes forward until his front is plastered against hers. He grips her chin and forces her head back to meet his gaze.

"Want to make a deal?" he asks.

She keeps her lips clamped shut and refuses to answer, so I prompt her. "Tick tock, little convict."

"What's the fucking deal?" she hisses.

"If your lying little cunt is drier than a nun's pussy, we won't touch you and will let you go." She sucks in a sharp inhale. I smirk behind my mask, knowing she is soaking wet. She always got off on me chasing her and holding her down as I fucked her.

"A-and... if it's not?" she stutters.

"Then we all get to take whatever the fuck we want from you." She gasps and snaps her head to the side at the sound of his voice, his red mask seems so ominous in the darkness.

"Do you agree?" I hedge as I release her wrist and force my hand behind her and Hux's bodies. I know that fucker isn't budging an inch because he wants me to feel how hard he is. I groan the instant my knuckles brush against his rock-hard cock, making him chuckle. Lennon trembles as I skirt my fingers along her thigh, then work my way back up to her pussy. She tries to push Hux away to get free, but he stands firm.

When I slide a finger through her folds, I groan. "You dirty little slut, you're drenched."

A sob tears out of her and she shakes her head as I start circling her clit. "Please..."

"Please what?" I push.

"Don't do this," she pleads.

"Revenge is a dish best served hot, little convict, and you stole years from us. I haven't felt the warmth of a tight cunt in nearly three years." He growls, her whole body turning to stone as she stares over at him.

"Kincaid..." she breathes out a moment before I push a finger inside her tight little pussy, pulling a scream from her and distracting her from that train of thought.

"Lift her, I want to taste that cunt." I withdraw my finger, bend down and grab her under her thighs, then lift her up so she is exposed and bare to my dad and Huxley. My boy drops to his knees and lifts his mask enough to expose his mouth. The sight of my boyfriend on his knees and eating my ex's cunt out is a sight I have dreamed of. Lennon cries out and arches her back as Hux laps at her pussy like a starving dog.

Dad stands there watching, he's stiff and I know how much strength he is using right now to remain where he is. We loved her. We wanted to protect her but she stabbed us in the back and stole my dad from me.

My dick is rock fucking hard and twitching in my jeans, begging for me to sink inside her tight little hole. Memories of her taking my virginity surface and I fight those fuckers not wanting to remember how good it once was between us. She begins to tremble in my hold, telling me without words that she is close and about to come all over Hux's face but, before she can tip over the edge, Dad speaks.

"Enough!" Hux does as he's told and pulls back. Len deflates against me but her body is coiled with need and she is pissed Dad just robbed her of her orgasm. "Strap her ass down. It's time she started paying us back for her sins."

She tenses in my arms as I push forward, move around Hux and past Dad to the dining room. She begins to thrash in my hold, forcing me to put her down, but I keep an arm around her waist so she doesn't run off when she sees the wooden table that is equipped with restraints.

"No! Please don't—"

I cut her off before she can finish. "This is happening, whether you like it or not. You had a chance to be free but that dirty little cunt of yours told us how much you wanted it, so you have no one to blame but yourself."

She makes a strangled sound in the back of her throat when I lift her feet off the ground and carry her over to the table. When I lay her down on the table I expect her to fight and scream but she does none of that. She just lays there glaring up at me with murder in her eyes, her upper lip peeled back in a snarl.

"Go. Fuck. Yourself." She announces each word. They are layered in disdain and malice, which brings a smile to my face.

"The only one who is getting fucked… is you," Dad snarls as he comes to stand at the foot of table and begins to shackle her ankles. Hux and I secure her wrists. She tries to fight but it's fucking pointless. She is no match for us. She will be at our mercy whether she likes it or not.

"Goddamn you!" she screams as she thrashes in her restraints. The three of us stand shoulder to shoulder and stare at her. She looks like a chained animal.

"God won't save you. He knows you're a sinner and *so do we...*" I growl. Hux laughs but there's a dark edge to it, he's been craving this moment for as long as we have. She's laid before us like a fucking feast ready to be devoured. Her pussy is showcased like a masterpiece painting that should be hung in a gallery. My mouth waters with the need to taste her cunt and feel her cum trickling down my chin as she screams.

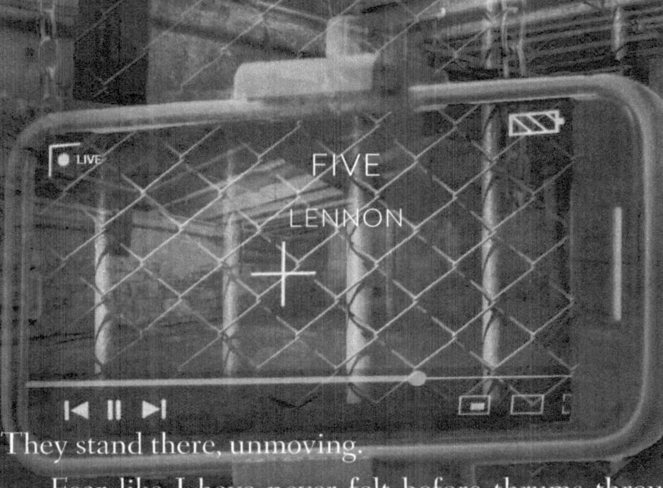

They stand there, unmoving.

Fear like I have never felt before thrums through me like a live wire, my emotions are all over the place, and I can't stop my pussy from throbbing with need. I want to cry, but I won't give these sons of a bitches the satisfaction of seeing how much they affect me or how truly terrified I am. I had every intention of plunging that knife into that purple-masked freak, but he was stronger.

I hate that I am weak and left at the mercy of these unhinged fucks. When they begin to move toward me, I start to panic and try to think of something to say to stop them from raping me.

The orange-masked guy snorts. "It's not rape if you're willing, little convict." I jerk back, shocked he was able to read my mind. "You still think out loud, little Lennon."

"Who the fuck are you freaks?" I yell as the red-masked bastard places his hands on my legs, sending heat surging through me. I try to fight my body's reaction but it's fucking useless, I'm a wanton whore and it's all because of how terrified I am.

Orange comes to stand on my left and purple is on my right. My breaths turn ragged as they slowly skate their fingers along my arms, sending gooseflesh dotting my skin.

"Your karma," the guy with the red mask answers. Even with the voice distorter I can hear the weight of those words and know there is a hidden meaning, but I have no idea what it is and why the fuck I am here. His hands glide up my legs and I fight not to shiver, but the moment he reaches the tops of my thighs and his thumbs graze my pussy, I tremble with need. He glides a thumb through my folds, and I'm powerless to stop the cry from tearing out of me.

The two men on either side of me laugh and it grates on my nerves, but I can't formulate words to snap at them when the guy pushes a single finger inside my wet cunt, forcing me to arch my back off the table.

"Such a greedy little slut, aren't you, little convict?" purple says as he pinches my nipple, drawing another sharp cry out of me. I tug against my restraints, which just causes orange to chuckle and grip my chin, forcing my head to the side to face him.

"You have enough holes for us to fill." My mind blanks of rational thought when the red-masked guy adds a second finger inside me. I tug against my restraints and arch my back off the table as I cry out. "Tell us how much you want our cocks."

I bite down on the inside of my cheek, refusing to answer. I don't want to give these assholes the satisfaction of knowing how much I want them to fuck me. To some this may seem crazy and fucked up but for me, this is a fantasy I have longed to fulfil. I *need* to experience three cocks inside me at least once in my lifetime. I want to be owned, dominated, used and controlled, but in order to give my full submission there must be trust, and we have none of that. I may be able to satisfy one part of my fantasy with having all my holes filled at once but that's it.

Orange places a hand over my eyes, darkness consumes me and I have no choice but to surrender to my other senses. Without my sight I feel like everything is heightened. When I feel a tongue slide through my slick folds, I scream so loud I fear the sound alone will cause the foundations of this home to crumble.

"Take it like a good little slut," one of them snarls a second before the cup of my bra is ripped down, then my nipple is sucked into a hot, wet mouth. I tremble with wanton need, my pussy weeping with the need to come. It's been so fucking long since I have felt the touch of a man and it shows from how quickly they can have me on edge and ready to explode.

"Can you feel that, little convict?" the man shielding my eyes says. "Do you feel his tongue circling that clit and his fingers inside your tight little pussy, forcing you closer to the edge?" I am panting and almost breathless, this is the most erotic experience of my life. "You want to come all over his fucking face, don't you?"

"Y-yes!" I rasp out as the other bites down on my nipple, making me scream.

"Keep being a good little whore and we might let you taste our cocks," he coos. The thought should repel me but in truth, all it does is make me more needy and wanton for the taste of them on my tongue. Before I can think more on his offer, a tidal wave of pleasure tears through me without warning. I come so fucking hard I am robbed of speech and air. I can't even make a sound as I arch off the table and squirt all over his face.

Only one man has ever been able to make me squirt but he left me when his father was sent to prison.

"What a good slut you are," he purrs as he releases my nipple with a pop. I can tell his mask is back in place without seeing him because his voice is robotic again.

I can't catch my breath because the other guy won't stop sucking on my clit and twirling his fingers inside me, drawing out my orgasm. I am powerless to stop my body from trembling and soaking the wood of the table with my cum. My skin feels tight, my nipples are so hard they could cut ice but, my pussy, it's primed and ready—no, begging for them to fill me with their cocks.

"S-stop," I plead.

"No one likes it when you lie, little convict," the one shielding my eyes says. "Now, be a good little toy and shut the fuck up and we might just give you what you are feigning for."

I shake my head, trying to deny what he says but the growl that reverbrates through my pussy tells me that the guy inflicting beautiful torture on my cunt knows I'm lying.

I war within myself for a minute. I know this is fucked up and wrong and I shouldn't be panting or wanting to beg them to fill all my holes, but that little monster inside me that has longed to be owned and dominated wants to throw caution to the fucking wind and embrace this moment while I have the chance. If these motherfuckers are gonna kill me, then the least they could do is make me feel alive and worshipped before they end me.

Surrender!

That one thought overrides everything and I choose to listen and unleash my inner temptress. I have kept her at bay for years since my stepbrother left me but not anymore. I am a bad bitch and it's time I stopped hiding her away. Stone ruined me for any other man. Kincaid hardened my heart to any man and I'm okay with that, but what I will no longer do is stop myself from chasing my sexual desires and hiding my wants from the world because I'm scared I will be judged.

"Fuck, don't stop. Make me come all over your face and then fuck me like the worthless whore I am." I hear the two guys groan and fight not to smirk, but the one with his face buried in my pussy stops and I almost want to whimper at the loss of his mouth.

"You get what the fuck we give you. You get the scraps of our attention when we offer it. You don't get a fucking say here."

My body turns to stone at the sound of his voice. I know that voice. I will never forget it for the rest of my life.

"Kin..." I breathe out as tears prick the backs of my eyes.

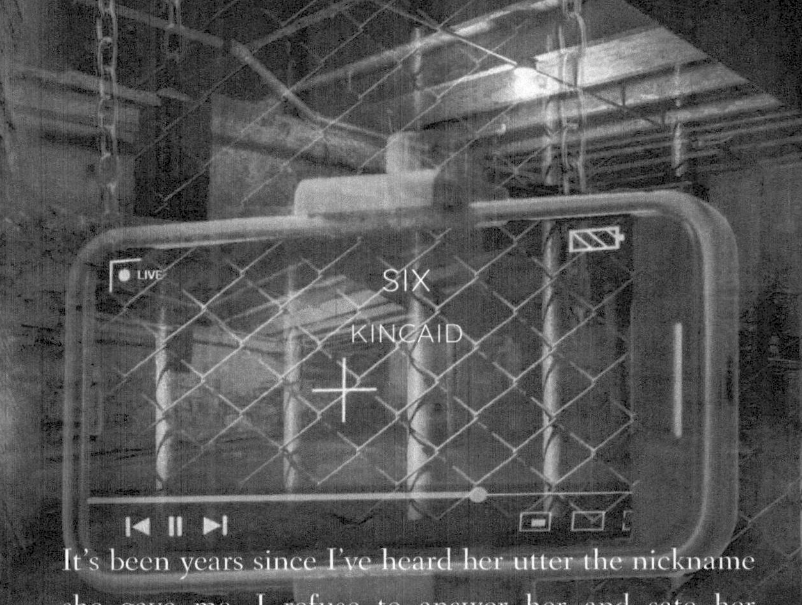

It's been years since I've heard her utter the nickname she gave me. I refuse to answer her and sate her intrigue, she deserves to wallow in uncertainty after what she did to me. She stole years of my life from me, took me away from my son because she refused to tell the fucking truth. She left me to fucking rot and broke my son and his boyfriend in the process.

I pull my mask down and look at Stone and Hux. Both of them nod, telling me they are with me and ready to take this to the next level. I reach for the machete that is leaning against the wall. I lift it and press it against her stomach. She tenses and fists her hands in the cuffs. She tries to move her legs but they won't budge. I look at Hux and nod, he removes his hand from her eyes and lifts her head so she can see what I'm doing.

As she sees the blade against her skin, she blanches and her eyes widen in terror at the sight of it. Her jaw slackens and she tries to shake her head but Huxley tangles his fingers in her hair and keeps her head in place. I glide the tip of the machete down her creamy skin, relishing how she shakes with fear.

A lone tear glides down her cheek and I grin behind my mask. Her bottom lip trembles as she fights back the sob from tearing out of her. As I reach the top of her pussy she loses the battle to hold back any sounds and whimpers. Stone laughs beside her but she keeps her gaze on me.

"Time is running out, little convict," my son taunts.

"Time for what?" she utters as I drag the blade down her pussy, applying enough pressure to scare her but not enough to draw blood.

"To escape your future. To return to the life you thought you could have without us," I answer. I press the tip of the blade against her inner thigh hard enough to draw blood. She thrashes in her restraints and screams out in pain as blood trickles down her leg. I groan at the sight of it. Reaching down I smear my hand through it and marvel at the sight of her soft skin turning red. My mouth waters for a taste. "Cover her eyes," I bark. Stone reaches out and places his hand over her eyes. She tries to shake her head and screams for him to stop but it's useless, we'll get our own way with her.

I push my mask to the top of my head and swallow the saliva pooling in my mouth before bending down and licking the trail of blood. I'm powerless to stop the moan that forces it's way out of me at the taste of her—she's so fucking sweet. Unable to hold myself back any longer, I flip the machete in my hand and the blade bites into my palm, but I feel nothing as I bring the hilt to her opening and push it inside her.

Her body grows taut at the invasion, but both Hux and Stone use their free hands to cup her tits and twist her nipples between their fingers and she moans. I press the pad of my thumb against her clit while pushing the remainder of the machete hilt inside her tight cunt.

"Fuck," she pants as I glide it almost all the way out before thrusting it inside her again. Her cry of pleasure reverberates off the walls and has both the boys groaning. I keep my pace even and steady to the point of it almost being torture. I see from the way she tries to grind down on the hilt that she wants it deeper—no, needs it deeper so she can come like a dirty little slut but I refuse to give her that satisfaction.

I want her begging and screaming for release, only then will I grant her that mercy.

"Please!" she cries out when I remove the handle as

soon as I feel her greedy cunt trying to clamp down on it.

"Beg me," I snarl.

She clamps her mouth closed, refusing to give me what I want so I keep going, knowing that she will crack soon and give me what the fuck I want. Her skin is flushed and a fine sheen of sweat coats her body. Lennon is a stubborn little bitch and it was one of the things I loved most about her, except for right now when I want her to give in. It's been years since I've felt the heat of a woman's pussy wrapped around my cock.

"Can you feel that, little convict?" Hux taunts. "Feel how good he can make that pussy feel without even sliding his cock inside you?" The moment it hits her, she silences her cries of pleasure and turns stiff on the table. I nod to Hux to remove his hand and allow her to see what I'm doing. The moment she does, her eyes widen to the size of dinner plates and fear shines in her eyes.

"Holy fuck, please—"

I cut her off before she can continue. "Please what, *slut*?"

She shakes her head and opens her mouth but no words escape. I continue fucking her with the hilt of the blade, relishing at the battle I see in her eyes. She tries to act like she isn't enjoying every fucking second of this. Her pussy is dripping and giving away how much she wants this.

"Oh God," she pants.

"That fucker can't save you," Stone growls.

"I-I... need..." She bites down on her lip and moans when I circle her clit with my thumb.

"You need us to let you come?" Hux supplies.

She whimpers and nods her head. "Yes," she grits out through clenched teeth. I smirk behind my mask.

"No," I growl.

She snaps her gaze to me and glares. "What?" she pants as I apply more pressure to her clit.

"Beg me for my cock like a good little slut," I snap and remove the hilt of the blade. Stone steps back and begins to unfasten his pants. I shake my head at the sight of Hux watching my son's every move. The second Stone's cock springs free, Huxley tries to move to him but I stop him with my words. "Untie her wrists." Hux fumbles with the straps for a second since he can't pull his gaze from my son's dick but he manages to get her free.

Huxley moves to stand in front of Stone and bats his hand off his cock and replaces it with his own. My boy lets out a long drawn out groan.

"Fuck," he growls.

"You like my hand on your cock, don't you?" Hux purrs in a robotic tone. I focus on Lennon. She's sitting up and watching their every move, not even trying to escape. She's always been a dirty bitch and I can't fucking wait to explore every inch of her body.

"I like your mouth better," Stone says. Len gasps but doesn't move an inch. Too focused on what they are doing, she misses me unclasping her ankles. Hux chuckles and lowers to his knees in front of Stone. Lennon waits for him to lift his mask, hoping to get a glimpse of his face, but before she can do that, I grip her ankles and yank her to me. She squeals in surprise but the sound is muted when she realizes I'm standing between her legs and there is nothing stopping me from taking her right here, right now, except for the thin material of my pants.

I stare up at him with my mouth ajar, when did he undo the restraints on my legs? It takes every ounce of strength I have not to peer back over my shoulder and take a peak when I hear the guy getting his dick sucked groan in pleasure.

"Beg me." My eyes widen at the guy in front of me. I shake my head, but then he snaps his hand out and grips my throat. His grip is tight enough to drive his point home but not enough to cut off my airways. "Don't fucking deny me, little convict. Beg for my cock and if you're a good girl, I might fuck you from behind and let you watch as those two fuck each other." His filthy promise is what tips me over the edge and has me throwing rational thought out the fucking window like it never existed.

"Please."

"Please what?" he pushes.

I suck in a sharp inhale and allow my inner bad bitch out. "Please fuck me so hard and deep I forget all about the fact you kidnapped me and locked me up and made me your fuck doll for the night."

"The fact you think this is a one time thing is fucking comical." Before I can process his words, he grips my waist, then spins me around so my feet are on the ground and I'm bent over the table. "Fuck him in front of her," he growls to the other two. I want to pout that I missed watching him getting his dick sucked as he pulls back and pushes the other guy's mask down, then helps him to his feet and leads him to the opposite end of the table.

My brain short circuits and I lurch forward when I feel the tip of his cock brush against my entrance. "You begged for this and now you will take it like a good little whore, am I clear?" he hisses from behind me. I'm too caught up in watching the other two in front of me. They are so comfortable with each other as they drop their pants. I almost choke on my spit when I watch the one who was getting his dick sucked drop to his knees behind the guy and start eating his ass. I'm jarred from my thoughts when the guy behind me spanks my ass and I yelp. "Answer me, bitch!" he roars.

"Y-yes, you're clear as crystal." I cringe at my jumbled words but I can't find it within myself to care,

I'm too focused on the two in front of me. I want a better view! The second the guy across from me groans, I whimper with need.

"Eyes on them as I fuck this used up cunt," he demands.

"Hmmm," I agree as I watch the guy climb to his feet and grip his cock in his hand—

"Fuck!" I scream out when he slams inside me. My pussy is burning and stinging with pain from the sudden invasion. I never expected him to be this big or to feel this full. God, he is stretching me so wide to accommodate his size, I haven't felt this full since... Stone.

"Fuck, you're so tight," he grits out from behind me as the two in front of us begin fucking, the guy thrusting so fucking hard the table shifts. "Take my dick like a good girl," he snaps, then draws back so only the tip remains inside me and then thrusts so hard and deep I cry out loud enough to wake the fucking dead. His pace is relentless and punishing to the point I can't focus. I can barely take a breath without feeling him invading every part of me.

"Look how good our little convict looks taking his cock, baby," one of the guys in front of me says. I can't decipher which one is speaking. All I can do is grip the edge of the table as I'm fucked like a whore by this savage behind me. He pushes me forward until I'm laying flat against the table, then lifts my right thigh to give him better access. When he thrusts inside me this time I scream, he feels so deep!

"She's taking your dad's cock like a good slut." I barely register his *dad* comment before another scream tears out of me when I feel a thumb shoved inside my ass. A hot flush works through my body. I'm fucking burning up but in the best way.

"Next time, you get the three of us at once," he growls from behind. I'm too delirious to process his words as I feel my orgasm building and latch onto that bitch with everything I have, needing this release more than my freedom right now. It crashes into me with such force it robs me of air. The scream that rips out of me rents the air with such power, I swear the windows shake. He pulls out in time for me to squirt all over his front before slamming back inside me.

He's relentless and doesn't ease his pace or allow me to come gently, he keeps fucking me like a starved man chasing his own release. If you mix the pleasure rolling through me plus the sounds coming from the two guy's fucking in front of me, I would say this is a dream. The sight of those two fucking like rabid dogs only serves to make my greedy cunt clench down on the cock inside me.

"Fuck, babe, I'm gonna come," the guy in front of

me growls. My breathing turns choppy as I wait with bated breath to watch this scene unfold in front of me.

"Do it, baby. I want to feel you inside me," the other encourages. My thoughts are derailed when the sweet spot inside me is hit again and a shudder rolls through me.

"Give me another orgasm," he demands from behind me. I shake my head but instantly stop when he pushes his thumb deeper inside my ass, making me scream. "Never deny me what I want," he roars.

"I can't," I cry out. The roar of release from the other end of the table snags my attention and I'm pissed I missed it.

"You two, get the fuck over here. Bux, put your cock in her mouth. Rock, on your knees and eat her cunt. I want one more orgasm before I fill this fucking cunt up." My eyes widen in shock as both of them scurry to do as he demands. I watch as the purple mask guy pulls out of the other and rushes toward us, dropping to his knees so he can fit beneath the table. The guy fucking me pulls me back enough so the other guy has access to my pussy.

The second I feel his tongue touch my clit I scream in pleasure. The orange masked guy climbs onto the table and scoots forward until his cock is right in my face. My mouth waters at the sight and without having to be prompted, I reach out and grip him in my hand, then wrap my lips around his head. The groan of pleasure from him only serves to empower me to the point I push back against the guy fucking me and grind down on the other's tongue, chasing my release like I'm owed it. And god-fucking-dammit, I am owed this shit and I *need* it. Orange's fingers tangle in my hair as he reclaims control and begins to fuck my face. I relax my jaw and breath through my nose so I can take him deeper.

Moans fall out of me like oxygen. I've never felt this sexy or unbreakable in my life. I have dreamed of a moment like this for so long and now that it's happening, I don't want it to fucking ever end.

"Fuck, she's sucking my cock so good I won't be able to last." His comment emboldens me. I hollow my cheeks, sucking him harder. Fuck, my senses are overloaded. I have a cock in my mouth and pussy, a thumb in my ass and a tongue circling my clit.

"She's close, I can feel her cunt tightening around my cock," he growls as his hold on my waist tightens. "She's gonna come for us like a good slut, then you can come all over her face while I fill this pussy with my release and mark the bitch as ours, finally."

The heat of her mouth wrapped around my dick is everything. Watching Kincaid fuck her like he owns her only serves to enhance my arousal. I just wish I was able to see Stone on his knees, eating her cunt. My grip on her hair tightens as I hold her in place and thrust into her mouth so hard she gags.

"Come on, you filthy little slut, I know you want to come." She flicks her eyes up and the sight of want reflected in them has me groaning. She moans around me and I shudder from the feeling of the vibration on my sensitive dick. "Come for them, convict, it won't be the last time you get fucked by my boyfriend and his dad." Her eyes widen for a split second in shock before Kincaid slams inside her with such force the table screeches along the ground. Lennon screams around me as her climax shreds her in half.

Kincaid doesn't stop fucking her. "I'm gonna come," he roars. I pull out of her mouth and jerk myself off. The dirty bitch is still coming down from her high but she pops her mouth open, wanting to catch every drop of my release. "Fuck!" Kin roars as he comes. I follow him over the edge as I come, jets of cum landing on her tongue, cheek and chin. Fuck me, it's a beautiful sight to see her marked with my release on her skin.

Aftershocks are still rolling through me as Kin pulls out of her. She's gasping and panting like she's just ran a marathon and in her defense, it must have felt like she just did. Kincaid didn't hold back, he kept to his word and fucked his revenge into her. Stone climbs to his feet with his mask securely back in place. Lennon flops forward and rests her forehead on the table trying to gather herself.

"Take her back to her cell," Kin barks as he tucks himself back into his pants and stalks out of the room. Stone shakes his head but leans forward and gathers her in his arms. She deflates against him and doesn't even put up a fight. I tuck myself back into my pants and follow after them. No one utters a word as we make our way into the basement. When Stone nears the cell, I see her stiffen in his hold.

Guilt churns inside me for a split second until I remember what her lie did to my family, she tore us apart.

I grab a pillow and a blanket from one of the shelves in the corner. When I make it back to the cell I find Stone standing in the entryway and Lennon is huddled into the far corner with her arms wrapped around her legs and her head resting on her knees. I brush past Stone, step into the cell and place the blanket and pillow beside her. She doesn't look up or even move as I back out, close the door and click the lock.

He and I turn to move away but her words have us both freezing. "I'm sorry. I never meant to hurt you or... *him*." Her tone is laced with guilt. She knows she lied but all we want is to hear her admit it. Look us in the fucking eyes and tell us *why*. We all loved her. None of us had a fucking right to want her but we did regardless. Lennon is a fucking vortex and sexy as sin, resisting her is harder than some would fucking think.

I feel Stone grow tense beside me. I remain silent, waiting for him to sort his thoughts and deal with her as he sees fit. "No idea what you're talking about. You're just some bitch we want to fuck." He attempts to take a single step but she has him halting when she speaks.

"And you were always the boy I wanted on top of me, but you hated the fact I wanted your daddy as well." Her cold, malicious tone has Stone growling and me feeling slightly proud. She actually had the balls to step up and taunt him.

Stone whirls around and faces her. She's still sitting in the corner but has her head held high like she has the upper hand here. "And where is your mommy again?" She reels back as if he hit her. "Hmmmm, you may think you know who we are, but the truth is, you are just as fucking clueless as the cunt you crawled out of. Make no mistake, little Lennon, you are here for a purpose. When we get what we want, we'll send your worthless ass home with nothing but memories of the time you spent here, thinking any of us gave a fuck about you."

When Stone storms out of the basement, I follow after him. My loyalty will always be with him, regardless of how I feel about Lennon. I'm about to follow him out the back door when Kin suddenly appears in front of me and cuts me off. I tear the mask off my head and glare at him.

"Let him cool off," he says.

I step back and shake my head. "He needs me."

"He always will, Hux, but you know that girl has always had the power to fuck with that boy's head. Let him get through this on his own and give him the chance to come to *you* for once."

"She knows who we are," I admit.

His brown eyes darken and suddenly from that one

look I see how he survived prison without any incident. Kin is a bad motherfucker and has a lot of pent up anger over being sent away for something he didn't do.

"It changes nothing," he grits out through clenched teeth.

I scrub a hand down my face and shake my head. "I'm down for anything, you know that. But I won't lose my family again because of her."

Kin reaches out, grips the back of my neck and pulls me forward until our foreheads are touching. "You boys will never lose me again. I swear it."

"She said *sorry*," I utter.

His grip on my neck tightens. "Don't let her in your head. This is about revenge. She needs to atone for her sins and that is why we are here. Once she admits the truth, she is free to go."

I nod my agreement. "I'll start setting up for the next event," I say as I pull out of his hold and head for the living room, but his words stop me.

"Don't let your love for her cloud your judgment, Huxley. Loving her is like loving a snake... it's only a matter of time before she strikes." His words are lathered in disdain and I get it. Truth is though, if I could have stopped loving Lennon St James, I would have done it years ago.

I keep my mind off her by focusing on my task of setting up the room. I have the three tripods set up with three seats behind them, we want to recreate her OnlyFans. We've been watching her for months and she had no idea.

I drag the twin size bed across the floor and situate it in the middle of the room, the red satin sheets and pillows are askew but I don't give a shit. She is going to put on a show for us and excitement is thrumming that I will be able to watch her put on a show for us in person. I want to smell her, touch her, feel her skin against mine.

Tick tock, little convict, your time is running out.

Sitting in this fucking cell for hours on end with crusted cum on my thighs and face is not my idea of a good time! They have come down here twice to serve me food and water. I wanted to refuse and tell them to fuck off but if I have any chance of getting the fuck out of here, I am going to need my strength and clothes! It's fucking freezing and all I have is a small throw blanket to ward off the chill.

I may not have been able to see their faces or hear their voices but I know it's them.

It has to be them!

The third guy has thrown me for a loop. I can't figure out who the fuck he is and it is starting to piss me off. I know for sure the one in the red mask has to be Kincaid, the purple mask is Stone, I am so sure of that fact but, who the fuck is in the orange mask?

"Tick tock, little convict, time for your show." I snap my head up at the sound of that stupid robotic voice and glare at the guy in the orange mask.

"Who the fuck are you?" I hiss from the corner of my cell.

"Convict, I can be a nightmare dressed as a day dream or I can just be your nightmare. I don't really give a fuck which one you choose."

"Fuck you," I spit as he comes to a halt in front of my cell.

"Get your sexy ass up. You need to shower before your show."

My brow furrows. "What show?"

His laughter sounds manic because of the mask and sets me on edge. "The one where we get to watch you get off before we fuck you." My mouth parts on a silent gasp. My mind is screaming at me to tell him to fuck off, but my pussy, that thirsty bitch, is quivering with need and clenching on air. "Let's go." I push to my feet as he opens the cell door. I take slow steps toward him, wary that at any moment he will try something. I eye him skeptically when he steps aside to allow me out of my prison cell. I gasp when he grips the back of my neck in a punishing hold, making me wince.

He uses his grip on me to lead me out of the basement. I shakily climb the stairs. Once we hit the landing, I look around and cringe at the sight of the dining room table. The shackles are still attached, but we don't head into that room, we veer off into the living room. I slam to a stop at the sight in front of me. Three cameras are set up with a direct view of the bed in the center of the room.

"Keep going," he growls from behind me and pushes me forward down the hallway. I try to look around and spot the other two guys, but they are nowhere to be seen. He shoves me into a room and I stumble forward, but catch myself on the edge of the basin. "Shower. Don't get any cute ideas, the windows are barred and I'll be waiting right here."

I shoot the fucker a scowl and attempt to grab the door so I can slam it in his face but he lurches forward and blocks my path.

"Door stays open, little convict." He tilts his head down to take in the sight of me and I suddenly feel exposed. "It's not like we haven't seen it before."

"Go fuck yourself," I hiss.

"I'd rather fuck you."

"In your dreams."

"I dreamt about my cock down your throat and that came true." I grind my teeth to the point of them hurting and spin away from him. I angrily tear my bra and panties off, tossing them to the side before climbing into the stall. I can feel his eyes on me the entire time. I turn the water to scolding hot and stand beneath the spray, not feeling the burn of the water. I help myself to the soap and shampoo. I take my sweet ass time, not caring that he is standing there waiting for me to finish. If they think I am going to take what they are dishing out without putting up a fight, clearly Stone and Kincaid have forgotten who the fuck I am.

When I finish, I step out of the shower and stand here naked and soaking wet, looking directly at him. I note the lights are shut off behind him now, but say nothing.

"Gonna offer me a towel?" I purr seductively. I feel his heated gaze on me, and as much as I try to deny the pull I feel toward him, I can't. It's the allure of not knowing who he is and the mystery that surrounds him that has me hot and needy.

Even with the mask on, I hear him gulp as he nods his head. He comes toward me, only stopping when there is a sliver of space between us. My breaths turn choppy and need courses through me. The light from his mask illuminates the rich brown of his eyes—something about them seems so familiar.

I'm pulled from my thoughts when he presses a towel against my chest. I frown. I didn't see him move.

"Your outfit is hanging behind the door. You have five minutes to get dressed." He doesn't say another word as he turns and stands in the doorway with his back to me, offering me some modicum of privacy. I want to snort at the audacity of the bastard but I manage to refrain... just. I peer behind the door, only for my fucking jaw to pop open at the sight of my white corset with the matching stockings and thong hanging there.

"You broke into my dorm room?" I grit out.

"Is it really *breaking in* if we have a key though?" the smug fucker tosses back at me. I want to stomp my foot like a petulant child but I refrain, just. I turn my back to the bastard and take my time dressing. This is one of my favorite outfits and something tells me they fucking knew that, which is why they picked it. Once I'm dressed, I turn to face him, only to see a pair of *my* heels dangling from his finger. I narrow my eyes but say nothing as I snatch them from him and slip them on.

"Happy?" I snap.

"Not yet but I will be when I get to bury my cock inside you." I balk at him but manage to refrain from snapping at him when he moves to the side and motions for me to lead the way. I take a step forward, ready to do as he asks but then stop in front of him. He stares down at me. Even with the low lighting I can see the hunger in his eyes. I tentatively reach out and place my hand against his chest. I don't miss the shiver that rolls through him at my touch.

Feeling emboldened by the fact he hasn't pushed me away, I close the sliver of space between us until I'm plastered against his front. I bite back my smirk when I feel how hard he is. I slide my hand between our bodies and relish in the sound of the hiss that escapes him when I cup his cock through his pants. I press up onto the balls of my feet and lick the side of his neck. A heady moan escapes me when I taste the salty flavor of his skin.

"Hmmmm, you taste good," I purr as I begin to stroke him. He's so big. His hands land on my waist, his hold bruising but I love it. I may not know who this guy really is but I know for a fact the other two are my stepdad and stepbrother, and they would never allow anyone to hurt me even after what I did to them.

"You keep rubbing my cock like that, convict, and we won't make your show," he growls.

Feeling impatient and over waiting for Hux to bring her ass in here, I stand from my chair and head down the hallway to see what the delay is, only to find the two of them in the doorway of the bathroom. Hux is pressed against the door jam with Lennon plastered against him while stroking his cock.

"You keep rubbing my cock like that, convict, and we won't make your show," Hux growls. Seeing the two of them together like this has me rock fucking hard just from the sight. Huxley tilts his head back and groans.

She licks a trail up his neck and moans. "I want to feel you inside me," she pants.

Unable to help myself, I push my sweats down and free my cock. I fist myself and bite back my hiss so they don't notice me. My eyes roll back when I begin to stroke myself, picturing her hand on my dick instead of my own.

"Get on your knees, little convict, and suck my cock, now." She obeys him like a good little slut. Seeing Hux be so dominant and in control is turning me the fuck on. I'm always the one in control when it comes to me and Huxley, he only submits to me. Seeing him take charge is fucking hot. I watch as she pulls his pants down and frees his cock. My mouth salvates at the sight of him.

"Fuck," she breathes out as she grips him in her tiny hand, then wraps her lips around his head. Hux groans loudly, then lolls his head forward to peer down at her, but then he catches sight of me. When his gaze locks onto mine I shiver. I can picture him smirking behind his mask. He knows this is a sight I have dreamed of seeing and now he is making it a reality. He tangles his hand in her hair and holds her in place as he begins to fuck her mouth.

"Harder," he snaps. Lennon thinks the command is for her but it isn't. I tighten my grip on my cock and pump myself faster to match his rhythm. She gags around him but he doesn't let up, he forces her to take every inch of him without mercy. Unable to contain it any longer, I groan out loud. I see her jolt in fright but Hux doesn't loosen his grip to allow her to see me. "You like watching her suck my dick, baby?"

"Yes," I grit out through clenched teeth.

"Good." He uses his grip on her hair to pull her back. She sucks in lungfuls of air as he looks down at her. "Crawl over to him and suck his dick while I watch." I expect her to put up a fight, instead she surprises us and nods. She drops onto her hands and knees and does exactly as he says and crawls to me.

Once she's kneeling in front of me, I release my hold on my cock and cross my arms over my chest. The bathroom light allows me to see the lust in her green eyes. It's been a long time since I have seen that look in her eyes and it's affecting me more than I want to admit. Huxley must sense the change in me because he comes to stand beside me against the wall.

"Suck his cock while you stroke mine," he barks. It's intriguing to see the shift in him when it comes to her, taking charge of the whole situation. Lennon nods, then shakily reaches out and grips me. I fight not to tense at her touch. But the second her lips are around my cock, I lose the battle and groan. For years I have longed to feel her lips wrapped around me again and now that it's happening, I can't focus on my revenge.

"Take him all the way," Huxley growls as she fists him and he tangles his hand in her hair, forcing her to take me deeper. She gags and splutters around me but Hux's grip on her keeps her in place, forcing her to breathe through her nose. A hiss escapes him when she starts pumping him in her hand. "Listen to her gagging on your dick, baby."

"It feels so good," I pant as she bobs up and down on my cock. Before I can get too lost in the feeling, she switches to sucking Huxley off while she strokes my dick. Fuck, I don't know what's getting me off more, the feeling of her hot mouth on my cock or watching her give my boyfriend head?

"Enough." At the sound of my dad's voice she pulls back and releases Hux with a wet pop, then turns her head to stare up at him. The glow of his mask is ominous, the red suits his hateful aura. "Get her ass in here now," he says, then stalks back to his chair in the living room. We help her to her feet and tuck ourselves back into our pants before we allow her to lead the way. Hux kills the bathroom light, plunging us into darkness. She heads straight for the bed without being prompted. Hux and I each claim our seats behind the tri pods with my dad sitting in the middle of us.

The only source of lighting is the glow from our masks. I hear her gulp audibly. None of us say anything as we wait to see what she will do.

"If you want a show from me then the least you can do is turn on a light," she says in a firm tone. Rather than answering her, Dad reaches out and unlocks his phone, then turns his flashlight on. Hux and I follow his lead and hit record on our phones.

"Follow our demands and you may just be reward-ed," Dad says.

"Rewarded how?" she presses.

"If it's a good enough show I may send you the video to upload to your OnlyFans so you can make a quick buck for being a slut." She flinches at Dad's words but says nothing, just nods her head. She moves around the bed, slides into the middle, then positions the pillows behind her so she's propped up. She closes her eyes for a minute, clearly trying to sort through her thoughts and find the courage to do what we are demanding of her.

When she opens them again, I can sense the shift in her. She's no longer tense and apprehensive. She looks like a vixen ready to bring us to the edge without even trying. She slowly glides her fingers down the center of her chest while keeping her gaze locked on my dad. When she cups her tits through her corset and moans, I have to bite down on the inside of my cheek to remain silent.

"Fuck," she moans when she pinches her nipple through the material. I fist my dick through my pants. When she continues to trail her other hand down her flat stomach, only stopping when she cups her pussy, I nearly leap out of my chair and throw myself at her.

She widens her legs, offering us a better view of her pussy when she pushes the material to the side. She glides a single finger through her folds and gasps when she pushes inside herself. Her back arches as she continues to finger fuck her pussy. I lean forward, wanting a better look but then she pulls her finger free and holds it up to show us just how wet she is. My mouth waters, needing to taste, but then the nasty bitch brings that digit to her own mouth and sucks it clean, driving me insane with that fucking move.

I whimper at the taste of myself. It's heady and tangy but so fucking good. I've shut off all rational thought and fallen back into my OnlyFans character that is a fucking sex goddess with no shame. I lean forward and slowly begin unbuttoning the corset, making sure to take as long as possible to egg these assholes on. When the final button is undone, I cup my tits, shielding them from their view just to drive them mad.

I can tell from the light of their masks that orange and purple have leaned forward to get a better view. Wanting to drive them crazy, I spin around so my chest is flat against the mattress and my ass is in the air with my pussy on full display. I smirk when I hear all of them groan at the sight. I lift slightly so I can fit my arm between me and the mattress, then begin swirling my clit and cry out. I'm so sensitive and ready to come from being over stimulated with sucking their cocks earlier.

I can still taste them on my tongue and it's driving me wild with need. "Your tongue feels so good," I pant. "I want your tongue inside my pussy," I call out as I continue to play with myself. I'm role playing and I know they are the three guys that book me every week for privates, it has to be them! "Yes! Just like that. You'll make me come, baby."

"Fuck yes, come for us, little convict," one of them calls out in that robotic tone. I ignore their plea and continue to play with my clit. To push them a little further, I sink a finger inside my dripping cunt and cry out.

"Oh, fuck yes. Tongue fuck my worthless pussy just like that, baby. I want to come all over that fucking face," I call out.

"What a good little slut you are," another one praises as I continue to fuck myself.

"I'm a dirty little whore, baby," I call back as I pull my finger free and circle my clit, driving myself mad with need. I begin to overheat and tremors start to roll through me. I'm so close and I know I'm about to soak this fucking bed with my cum. Knowing they are not only watching but recording me is fucking hot. Unable to hold my orgasm any longer I surrender to it. I'm so mindless with need as it rolls with me I scream his name. "Kincaid!"

Before I have a chance to even finish coming down from my high someone leaps on top of me, knocking the air from my lungs and flattening me against the mattress. His weight on top of me makes it hard to breathe. I start to panic and thrash beneath him but it's no use, he's too strong.

"Say that name again and I'll rip your fucking tongue out and fuck you with it." I still beneath him. I may not be able to hear his real voice but even in that robotic tone I can tell his threat isn't empty.

"I'm sorry," I whisper breathlessly. I wait for him to scold me further but to my surprise, one second his weight is on top of me, then in the next it's gone. I roll over only to find the three of them standing at the end of the bed looking right at me. Orange and purple both have their cocks in their hands while red stands in the middle, oozing tension out of every pore of his body.

"You have two choices," orange says.

I dart my tongue out to moisten my lips before I ask. "What are they?"

"Get on your knees and suck our dicks or—"

Red cuts orange off before he can finish. "You take all three of us now." My eyes widen, but not from fear but from excitement.

"Option two!" I call back without hesitation. None of them say anything for a moment, and I begin to worry that they were just fucking with me, until purple moves to the side of the bed and strips off his pants. I gasp in shock when orange tosses him something that he manages to catch. When he pops the top and I hear him squirt something into the palm of his hand I realize it's lube.

This is really about to happen!

My breathing turns choppy as anticipation rolls through me. I only dreamed of ever being able to have Stone and Kincaid at the same time and now, it's finally about to come true. I just wish more than anything that they would lose the masks and reveal themselves to me. I know I fucked up so badly and I wish I could take it back, but I can't.

I have been living with the guilt of my lie for years.

"Turn over." I do as Stone says and lay flat against the bed. He grips the waistband of my thong and peels it down my legs. "You filthy bitch, you destroyed these." My pussy clenches on air. "It's fucking soaked," he tells the others, then tosses my ruined thong to Kincaid who brings it to his mask and inhales. I frown. Can he really smell through that thing? My mouth parts on a silent gasp when he hands it off to orange, who stuffs it in his pocket. I startle when Stone parts my cheeks and I hear him spit before I feel it hit my asshole.

I shiver when he begins to swirl his finger around my hole, a moment later I hear him squirt the lube then shiver when I feel the coldness of it hit my crack. He lathers my hole a second before he begins pushing a finger inside. I lurch forward at the intrusion but he uses his other hand to grip my leg and keep me in place.

"Get on your hands and knees," Kincaid barks. I follow his instructions while Stone continues to prod my tight muscle wall. My eyes nearly bug out of my head when I watch orange rid himself of his pants, then slide onto the bed and shuffle toward me. "Climb on top." Stone releases his grip on my leg but doesn't remove his finger from my ass as I climb on top of his friend. His head is falling off the side of the bed but he doesn't seem to care.

"Put my cock inside you, convict." I shakily reach between us to do as he ordered but I freeze when Stone pushes a second finger inside me, making me scream. The burn is fucking real. "Breathe, the more you fight it, the worse it will be." I stare down at the stranger beneath me and try to do as he says. I breathe through the pain and line him up with my entrance, trying to focus on the feeling of him sliding inside me rather than Stone fucking my ass with his fingers. He's so big, he's stretching me out so fucking good I can't stop the sounds tumbling from my lips as

I sink down on him, taking every fucking glorious inch.

"Fuck, she looks so good taking your cock, baby," Stone says from behind me. I almost whimper with relief when he withdraws his fingers from my ass but then I feel the bed dip under his weight and turn to peer over my shoulder. He places his hand on my back and pushes me until I am laying flat against orange's chest. He wraps his arms around me, holding me in place as Stone parts my ass again. Unable to stop myself, I tense when I feel the head of his cock pressed against my forbidden hole.

"I've never done this before!" I blurt.

"I know," Stone says as he presses forward, pulling a scream of anguish from me. He pauses, allowing me to adjust but it hurts so much.

"I can't!" I plead and shake my head but a yelp escapes me when my head is ripped up by my hair and I'm forced to meet Kincaid's stare.

"You'll take what the fuck we give you and then thank us for it, because that's what a good whore does, isn't that right, little convict?"

I must take too long to answer before orange adds, "Tick tock, little convict."

I hold Kincaid's stare and pluck up every ounce of courage I have as I answer. "I'll take everything you have to give if it means I get *you*."

My grip on her hair tightens as her words sink in.

I knew she was smart but she put together who we are quicker than I would have liked. I knew she had feelings for me but I never knew how deep those feelings ran until now. I'm pulled from my turmoil when Stone thrusts inside her, drawing a blood curdling scream from her. Tears roll down her cheeks and I shoot my son a fucking glare.

The little prick shrugs his shoulders while Lennon is whimpering quietly. The sight of her in pain and shedding tears isn't bringing me satisfaction like I thought, it's pissing me off and making me want to break my own kid's jaw for hurting her.

"Breathe, convict. When you adjust, it will feel so good, I promise," I find myself saying without meaning too. She looks up at me with so much trust in her eyes that it angers me and I forget all about her being in pain. I release my hold on her hair, then push my pants down to free my cock. Her mouth parts at the sight of it, the pain that was present a second ago in her eyes has vanished and is replaced by need.

"Move," Hux barks. Stone does what he says and pulls almost all of the way out of her before thrusting forward. Lennon cries out but this time there is pleasure mixed with the pain. I step forward, widening my stance so Huxley's head is between my legs. I'm blocking her view of him now but she doesn't seem to notice. Lennon doesn't wait for me to say anything, she just opens her mouth giving me access. When she wraps her lips around my cock I throw my head back and groan.

I've only had the pleasure of feeling her mouth on me once and this feels better than what I remembered. The girl is fucking skilled to put it mildly. I almost lurch back a step when I feel Hux grip my ass. I know what he's about to do and I should tell him to fuck off but I don't. I hear his mask hit the floor a second before he parts my ass, then I feel his tongue prodding my hole. A groan slips out of me at the same time Lennon moans around me.

"Her ass is so fucking tight," Stone grits out as he thrusts into her, making her cry out. She's surrendered to her pleasure and pushing back against him now while grinding down onto Hux. When he groans the vibrations against my asshole has me trembling. An animalistic sound escapes me when he pushes his tongue inside me.

"Deeper!" I snap. Lennon and Huxley both obey my demand. She takes me all the way into the back of her throat. He buries his face in my ass and tongue fucks me like a rabid dog. The feelings these two are eliciting inside me are fucking hard to explain. My mind is blank, my need for revenge against her is muted as I get lost in the feelings they are making me feel. Lennon reaches out and grips my waist, pulling me in closer so she can have better access.

"Hmmmmm," she cries out around me when Hux meets her thrust. "Ahhhhh," she cries out when Stone and Hux thrust inside her at the same time. "Hmmmahhhh," she cries again, then starts shaking uncontrollably and I growl my approval at the sight of her coming. She is limp and trembling but we're not done with her yet.

"I'm gonna come!" Stone snaps and thrusts inside her twice more before he's throwing his head back and roaring out his release. As much as I want to come down her throat I can't. I want her ass and pussy filled with our cum!

"Close your fucking eyes," I snap at her. She obeys my command. I step back, then bend down and grab

Hux's mask and secure it on his face before moving around the bed. Stone chuckles at the sight of me, but pulls out of her and steps aside, giving me access. She gasps when she feels me behind her. I don't give her any warning as I line my dick up and thrust inside her ass. She screams but not from pain, this time it's all pleasure.

"Yes, fuck, please don't stop," she begs as Hux and I fuck her. I match my thrusts with his, making sure she can feel every inch of our cocks.

"Take our cocks, convict," Huxley shouts.

"Yes, give it to me. I fucking need it," she pants as she presses back against my chest. I reach around her and cup her tits in my hands, loving the feeling of how perfectly they fit me.

"Play with her clit, I want to watch her come," Stone demands. Huxley obeys his boyfriend without hesitation. She instantly begins to tremble in my hold and I know she is seconds away from climaxing.

"Get there, I want to come with her," I snap.

"I'm close," Huxley grits out.

"Oh God!" she cries out.

"Don't waste that man's time, he isn't coming to save you," Stone remarks.

"Now!" I roar. The three of us come in unison. The sounds of all our cries saturate the room and the stench of sex is pungent in the air, but I've never smelled anything so fucking good in my life. When I manage to get my breathing under control, I pull out of her. She flops forward onto Hux, making him grunt.

"Sorry," she mutters, barely above a whisper.

"Take her back to her cell," I order.

"No," she says with such conviction I whirl around to face her. She lays there with her eyes closed like she is the one calling the fucking shots.

"The fuck did you just say?" I snarl.

She blinks her eyes open and looks tiredly at me. "I need a second. If he pulls out of me right now I'm about to squirt all over him and this bed." Realization dawns on me. When she came, Hux never pulled out of her to allow her to come properly.

Intrigue propels me.

"Show us." Her eyes widen in shock.

"What?"

"Either you move on your own or we do it for you," I fire back.

She cringes then pushes up enough to look down at Hux. "Sorry, big guy," she whispers. When she lifts up and his cock slips out, sure enough she was telling the truth. She comes all over him, making him choke on the air beneath her. Stone and I stand here staring at her silently. When she finally manages to stop, she climbs off the bed and crosses her arms over her chest and rests her chin down in shame, which just pisses me off.

I march over to her, grip her chin in my hand and force her head until she meets my gaze. Shame and anger swirl in her green eyes.

"Don't ever hide that shit from us again. You don't get to feel shame over what you just did. We fucking love it and you *will* be doing that again for us tomorrow."

Surprise etches into her features. "You like that?"

"No. I fucking love it."

Color tinges her cheeks. "I didn't think—"

"You aren't here to think." She tries to reel back but I tighten my grip, making her wince while holding her in place. "You're here until we say otherwise. You will do as you are fucking told."

She inhales sharply. "Okay," she whispers.

"Where was this submission when it was needed years ago?"

My response has tears filling her eyes. "I didn't mean to hurt you," she urges.

I release her with a shove and she stumbles back a step. "In order for you to have hurt me, I would have had to care," I spit back at her.

Stone and orange have brought me food and water but I can't stomach it. After what Kincaid said to me last night, my stomach has been in knots. When they brought me down my second meal and saw I hadn't touched the first one or the water, they dragged me upstairs and told me to shower. I did so on autopilot without really thinking. I was surprised when they gave me a shirt and some sweats to wear. The clothes are too big for me but I didn't complain even when they locked me back up with orders to eat and drink.

Hours later and I still can't stomach the thought of eating. I need them to let me explain. If they would just listen then they would know I didn't have a choice. I never meant to hurt either of them but she didn't give me a choice! I hate my mom, I'm not sad the bitch is dead. She deserved to OD in her fucking shitty trailer on her own with no one around her.

I snap my head up when I hear the cell door unlock and frown when I don't see any of them around. I push to my feet, cautiously move toward the door and push it open, expecting one of them to jump out any second but they don't.

I debate trying to escape like I did the first night but push that thought aside almost instantly. Running hasn't done me any good and now that I have them back in my life, I don't want to lose them again. I take a deep breath and push all my emotions away. If the only way I can have them is physically then so-fucking-be-it.

I yank the shirt off and strip off the sweats. I toss the clothes back into my cell and ignore the chill in the air as I make my way through the basement. When I reach the stairs I see the door at the top is slightly ajar. I keep my wits about me as I climb the steps as quietly as I can. When I slowly push the door open and peer out I see nothing but darkness. I step out and the hairs on the back of my neck instantly stand on end, my breathing turns choppy and my palms start to sweat.

I inch my way past the living room and find it empty. It looks exactly as it did when I left it yesterday. I creep into the dining room and find that vacant as well. My eyes widen when I spot the back door in the kitchen wide open. I stand here just staring at it until I hear something dragging along the hardwood floor behind me. I whirl around and shriek at the sight of Kincaid in his red mask with an axe dragging behind him.

I don't think.

My flight or fight instincts kick in and I turn and run.

The cold air bites into my skin, the snow beneath my feet burns but I don't stop. I'm naked and terrified. The moon is my only source of light. I look around and see nothing but trees!

I'm in the middle of the fucking woods!

"No one will hear you scream, convict." I scream and snap my head to the right to see orange leaning against a tree with a fucking baseball bat resting on his shoulder. I veer left to avoid him. I can feel Kincaid gaining on me but I don't look back. I don't feel the cold or exhaustion, my adrenaline keeping me going. Rationally I know they won't hurt me but I can't fight against the need to run and get away.

I hear their boots crunching in the snow behind me. I know they are getting closer but I refuse to give up. The air is knocked out of me when something tackles me from the side. I land in the snow with a grunt. I gasp for air but I can't breathe from the weight on top of me.

I look up to see Stone in his purple mask. He

shifts so he is straddling me. I try to push him off but freeze when he presses a knife against my throat. Unfiltered terror rolls through me. I see Kincaid and orange out of the corner of my eye come to a stop beside us, but I don't dare move a muscle or take my gaze off Stone.

"You caught our little convict," orange says. Even with the fucking voice distorter I can hear the humor in his tone which pisses me off.

"Stone, please—"

He cuts me off by pressing the blade into my skin. I hiss in pain. "You don't get to say my name." I knew it was them but hearing him confirm it hits me harder than I thought it would. Tears prick the backs of my eyes.

"Get her ass up," Kincaid orders. Stone remains where he is for a minute before growling, then pushing off me. The moment he is off me all the adrenaline drains out of me and I instantly feel the sting of the snow against my skin and the bite of the cold. I was stupid to run out of the house naked. Orange leans down, grabs my arm and yanks me to my feet. In a move so bold he doesn't expect, I whirl around and smack the mask off his face.

My jaw slackens at the sight of his face. I know the other two are Stone and Kincaid but I had no idea who this guy was until now.

"What the fuck!" I hear one of the other two snap behind us, but I can't tear my gaze from his.

"Don't look so surprised, little convict," he taunts.

I shake my head as I stare up at him in shock. "Huxley Verlies," I breathe out.

He smirks down at me. "I'm surprised you remember who I am." My brows bunch in confusion but he pushes on. "Knowing who I am doesn't change shit."

"Why are you doing this?" I push as he grips my arm and begins dragging me toward the other two, who are standing by a tree.

"Because you didn't just break their hearts, you broke mine as well." His honesty floors me. I never in a million years thought I would ever see Huxley again. He and Stone were best friends. He knew about me and Stone and never judged us. Which is why, the night Stone came to me and asked me if I would be the one to take Huxley's virginity, I agreed. I was always attracted to Hux. Anyone with fucking eyes would be but I never thought he saw me as anything more than Stone's stepsister.

He shoves me forward and I stumble into Kincaid, forcing him to drop his axe in order to catch me. I can't feel my toes and my shivering has worsened but they don't seem to care. When Kincaid shoves me away from him my back slams into a tree and I whimper in pain. Stone suddenly appears in front of me. I stare up at him, waiting for him to help me or take me back to the house so I can warm up, but instead he reaches behind him and pulls out a rope, then tosses it to Huxley.

The cruel look in his eyes has tears clouding my vision. Huxley claims Stone's spot and begins tying my hands. I don't fight him or try to pull away. I keep my head down as he grips my restraints and pulls me forward until I'm flush against his front. As crazy as it sounds, it was easier to look at him with his mask on. The sight of his face forces me to remember the past and I hate thinking about that.

"Tonight, you had the chance to run and escape us but failed," he says smugly, the sound of his voice has me flinching. "What do you think your punishment should be?"

I shake my head. "I—d-d-don't... know," I stammer. My teeth are chattering and making it hard to talk. I'm so fucking cold!

"I'll tell ya what, if I slip a finger inside your cunt and find you dry, I'll carry you back to the house and put you in the sauna to warm up." I whimper wanting what he's offering.

"But, if you're wet, we're fucking you right here, right now." I snap my head and look at Kincaid with wide eyes.

"I'll die of hypothermia out here!" I snap.

The bastard just shrugs.

When Hux grips the back of my neck I turn back to him and hate the sight of the knowing smirk on his face. I know it, he knows it and so do the other two that I'm wet. It's no fucking secret I get off on fear. Rather than allow these fuckers the upper hand I take control and widen my legs, making Huxley's brows raise in question. I lean back against the tree and push my pelvis out to him.

"The least you could do is offer me a bit of warmth and use your tongue rather than your cold fingers, don't ya think?" I suggest seductively. To drive my point home, I lift my arms above my head and rest them back against the tree, offering them the illusion that I'm restrained. Hux groans, then looks to Stone and Kincaid. I keep my focus on Huxley but I can feel the others' stares boring into me. "Come on, baby, get on your knees and taste how much I want you," I hedge. Suddenly the cold is forgotten as I begin to heat with want. I know come tomorrow I'll probably have the worst cold but I don't care, it will be worth it.

"Fuck it," Huxley mutters as he steps forward and drops to his knees in front of me. Just when he is about to lean in I stop him with a toe to his chest, drawing his eyes to mine.

"I want you to put me on your shoulders and eat

my pussy while they watch." He nods like a puppet, forcing me to hide my triumphant smirk. Hux lifts my legs and places them over his shoulders, then stands. The rough bark bites into my cold back but the pain vanishes the second he buries his face in my pussy. I throw my head back and cry out in pleasure. Remembering that I am on mission here, I force myself to focus and not get lost in the feelings he is electing from me. I turn my gaze to Stone, knowing he will be easier to crack than his father. "His mouth feels so fucking good on me," I purr.

"Shit!" he hisses and shakes his head, then turns away defeated. They may have started out thinking they had won the battle but I'm about to win the fucking war and force the three of them to crave me.

I loll my head to the side and look directly at Kincaid and moan when Huxley sucks my clit into his mouth. "Kin, he's eating my pussy so fucking good, I'm so wet for him," I taunt.

"Fuck this. Carry her ass inside, she's getting punished for this fucking stunt!" His sinister promise has me shivering but not from the cold this time.

Forgive me father for I am so ready to sin with my daddy... again.

FOURTEEN

HUXLEY

I stomp back toward the house with her thrown over my shoulder, her skin is ice cold and she's turning purple. As I near the back of the house I make a last minute decision and bank left. I expect to hear Kincaid and Stone yelling for me to head inside but they say nothing as they follow me toward the sauna. Don't get me wrong, we all want revenge for what she did, but we also would be liars if we said we didn't care about her well being and right now, she is freezing and needs to warm the fuck up.

I was in the sauna earlier and left it running. In hindsight it was good thinking on my part. I place her on her feet in front of the door and grind my teeth at the sight of her shivering. Her lips are blue and her skin is a hue of purple.

"Get your ass in the fucking sauna, now!" I snap.

Her eyes widen at the anger in my tone but she doesn't argue. She shakily pulls the door then steps inside, closing it behind her. I turn to face Kincaid and Stone. Kin stands there with his arms crossed over his chest, making me roll my eyes. "If she dies or loses some fucking toes then that is on you. I refuse to have a part in that shit."

"She has you pussy whipped," Kin spits out. I glare at the fucker.

"Correction. She has all of us pussy whipped. Look at where the fuck we are, Kin. We're in the mountains, hiding out in a cabin your grandfather left you. You aren't any better than us. I may have feelings for her but so do both of you!" I focus on Stone who is standing there with his head down. I step forward and grip his chin, forcing him to look at me. I remove the mask from his face and look into his blue eyes that hold so much anger. "I love you." He sucks in a shuddering breath.

"I love you too," he says quietly.

"But, we both love her too." He opens his mouth to argue, no doubt, so I push on. "Baby, you and I have been in love with that girl since we were teenagers. Yes, we are both pissed for what she did to your father, but look where we are, Stone. We did all of this under the ruse of revenge but the truth is, you don't fuck someone you hate and want to torture."

Stone stands there staring at me with confusion written all over his face. He isn't the type of guy to confess his feelings or leave love notes. He's the type to just assume you know how he feels and right now he is torn between his heart and his loyalty to his father. I run my fingers through his black hair and smile reassuringly before turning to Kin.

Before I can say a single word he speaks. "She stole years of my life. You two can forgive her but I'm not done torturing her." Kincaid doesn't wait for us to respond before he brushes past and enters the sauna. Stone sighs, then grips the front of my hoodie, pulling my focus back to him. His eyes are filled with lust and that look alone has me wanting to devour every fucking inch of him.

"Just because I want her doesn't lessen my want for you." A smirk tugs at the corner of my lips. I lean in until there is barely a sliver of space between us.

"Baby, your ass will always belong to me but I'm good with sharing our cocks with her." He laughs but it's quickly cut off when we hear Lennon scream. Both of us rush into the sauna only to come to a halt at the sight of Kincaid naked except for his mask, sitting on the bench with Lennon on his lap, her legs spread wide, showing us her pussy while his cock is buried in her ass.

"I changed my mind, she isn't the one being

punished, you two are." When Lennon locks eyes with Stone I frown, until I realize this is the first time she is seeing him without his mask on. The lighting in here gives us a clear view of the longing in her eyes as she stares at him.

"Stone," she mutters.

"Bounce up and down on my cock while they watch," Kin barks. Lennon is too lost in her head to hear a word he said. Kin growls, then fists her hair in his hand and yanks her head back at an odd angle so she can look up at him. "Unless you want to be chained to a fucking tree, you will move that ass and give me what the fuck I want."

"I'll give you what you want and even put on a show for them, all you have to do is let me take control, *Daddy*." My brows hit my hairline. Stone chokes on fucking air. We cut a glance at each other in shock before turning back to them. Kincaid just stares at her for a minute straight. I expect him to tell her to shut the fuck up and do as she's told, but he suprises us both when he releases her hair.

"Make it good or that ass is mine again," he warns.

"What's my limits?" she counters as she eases off him and turns her back to us so she can look down at him.

"Mask stays on," he answers.

She peers over her shoulder at us and smirks before

looking back to Kin. She seductively lowers herself onto his lap but doesn't lower onto is cock. "Touch my tits, Daddy." I bite back my groan, this fucking girl is a goddamn temptress! Age has not diminished my attraction to her, if anything it has only fucking heightened it. Kin cups her tits in his hands. She throws her head back and moans. "Pinch my nipples." He does as she says. The cry of pleasure that tumbles from her lips has me and Stone groaning—my cock is so fucking hard it's painful.

"Suck my dick," I grit out. Stone reaches for me only for his dad's words to have him freezing mid way.

"No! You fuckers get to watch and not touch each other." I shoot the motherfucker a glare.

"The fuck?" I snap.

Lennon reaches between them and lines his cock up with her pussy and slowly sinks down onto him. I watch every inch of him disappear inside her tight little cunt. Kincaid being the bastard he is doesn't make a sound, he wants her to think she doesn't affect him.

"Yes!" she pants when he is balls deep inside her. The little slut looks back over her shoulder at us and smiles. "Fuck, he feel so good inside me."

"Tell us how good he feels?" Stone throws back.

She rises onto her knees, then slams down onto him, her scream bouncing off the walls of the sauna, making me shiver with need. The urge to grip my cock is strong but I fight against it. Edging is fucking hot if it's done right and so far she is doing a fucking good job of driving me insane with need.

"Soooooo, good," she cries out as she bounces up and down on him. "His cock is so big. I feel so full." I inhale sharply through my nose and clench my fists at my sides. It's taking every ounce of strength I have to remain where I am.

"You take my cock like a good slut," Kin praises. "Who do you belong to, little convict?"

I snarl, the cunt is going to make her say his name. I see Stone tense beside me, expecting her to say the same thing but she doesn't.

"The three of you, Daddy. I'm all of yours."

I'm so hot, sweat is dripping off me but I don't care. I feel every inch of Kincaid inside me and this is better than any dream I have ever had of him fucking me. His hands on my tits, pinching my nipples, is sending my mind whirling. I feel my pussy quivering and ready to come, but I don't want to come yet so I lift off him. Before he can say anything, I spin around so I'm facing Stone and Huxley, then reach behind me, grip his cock and line it up with my ass, then slowly sink down onto him.

The burn is fucking real but I push through it, knowing this is going to be euphoric for us both. When he bottoms out inside me, we both moan at the feeling. I reach back and grip his arms, then place his hands on my tits and hold them there as I grind against him while staring directly at Stone and Huxley.

Both of them look murderous and ready to rip Kincaid apart for making them watch this, but for me, this is the hottest fucking thing I have ever done and it is only fueling my need for the three of them to be inside me.

"Fuck, you feel so good," I moan as Kin thrusts into me.

"Take my cock, you filthy slut," he hisses in that robotic tone. I wish more than anything he would take his mask off like Stone and Hux.

"Give me everything you got, Daddy," I say as I slam down onto him and cry out. "Yes, you're making my cunt so wet." Huxley groans and throws his head back to stare at the roof. I stop grinding on Kin and ignore his growl of warning as I look at the other two. "He said you couldn't touch *each other*, he never said you couldn't touch me," I breathe out. I almost laugh out loud when their jaws unhinge. It takes a second for my invite to sink in, then they are tearing their clothes off like their asses are on fire.

"You'll pay for that," Kincaid says, low enough for only me to hear. I lean back against his chest and look up at him.

"I'll pay however you want me to as long as you don't leave." Before he can answer, Stone steps between my legs and lifts them, until my heels balance on the edge of the bench seat, I shiver at the sight of him licking his lips while staring at my pussy. Huxley stands on the bench beside us with his dick in his hand, my mouth waters at the sight of his beautiful cock.

"I'm gonna fuck you so hard, I'll leave an imprint of my cock inside you," Stone vows. I open my mouth, urging Hux to fill it without words. He obliges. At the same time, Stone thrusts inside me without warning, making me scream around Hux's girth. "Fuck, she's so tight."

"Look at how good she looks with us filling all her holes. Isn't she a good little whore?" Kin says. His praise has me shivering and wanting to please him. It takes me a minute to find a rhythm. I match my thrusts with Stone's and bob up and down on Huxley's dick. He's crouching down to give me better access. I know the position isn't ideal for him but he isn't complaining.

When Stone hits that fucking sweet spot inside me I choke on Hux and begin gagging so badly he pulls out of my mouth. I flop back against Kin and suck in lung-fuls of air.

"Now, that wasn't nice," Hux scolds Stone, who smirks at him until Huxley fists his hands in Stone's hair then yanks his head forward and slams his dick inside his mouth. My jaw slackens at the sight and need like I have never felt before erupts inside me at the sight of them.

"You like having Stone's cock inside you while Huxley sucks his cock?" Kincaid hedges.

I swallow audibly and nod. "Yes," I answer, then moan when Stone plunges inside me with so much strength Kincaid grunts. "Fuck me like that!" I scream out. Stone does as I ask and within seconds I'm clawing at his bare chest and screaming as my climax slams into me without warning, Stone pulls out of me in time for me to squirt all over his front.

"Fuck, that shit is hot. Do it again, but next time I want my mouth on her cunt so I can taste it." Huxley's words have my eyes widening in surprise. I don't get lost in my thoughts thanks to Stone pushing inside me again and short circuiting my brain. Having him and his dad inside me at the same time has me feeling so full and out of my mind with fucking lust. Seeing Huxley fuck Stone's face is better than watching porn. It's so hot to see two men so comfortable with their sexuality that they don't give a fuck who is around to see.

I feel like Jello. I'm wrung out and spent, but neither of these two seem to care. Kin is gripping my hips and is lifting me up and down to meet them thrust for thrust. My throat is dry and hoarse from screaming but I have never felt more alive in my life.

Huxley surprises me when he pulls free of Stone's mouth then jumps off the bench and comes to stand behind Stone. I watch with bated breath as he pushes Stone forward, until he is flush against my chest. I can't focus on what Hux is doing with Stone being this close to me. His lips are so close to mine and I'm starving for a taste of him. I don't overthink it as I lean forward and seal my mouth to his. He freezes and I think for a second that he is going to push me away, but then I feel his hand tangle in my hair and hold me in places as he forces his tongue inside my mouth and groans. I open for him and melt into Kincaid as Stone explores my mouth familiarizing himself with my taste again.

"Fuck!" We break apart at Huxley's shout. I stare open mouthed at the sight of Hux standing in front of me with his cock buried in Stone's ass. When he pulls back then slams forward I cry out. Kincaid and Stone both grunt. "I'm not gonna last," Hux admits as he continues to fuck Stone like a frenzied beast. His thrusts are harsh and hard, but fuck it feels so good.

"Keep fucking her, I'm gonna cum!" Kincaid shouts, Hux is turning red as he tries to fight off his release. I feel my own brewing again and I just know this orgasm will split me in half.

"I'm close, baby," Stone calls out.

"Get there, I can't... hold on," Huxley grits out through clenched teeth.

"Holy shit!" I cry out.

"Fuck!" Kincaid roars as he comes inside me, filling me with his release.

"I'm coming!" Hux bellows.

"Yes!" Stone cries out at the same time as Hux, and they both come together. Seeing them fall apart is fucking beautiful. I expect them to pull out and not worry about me, but to my surprise, Hux pulls out of Stone then yanks him back. He slips out of me, then Huxley drops to his knees and pushes two fingers inside me making me scream and arch off Kincaid who wraps his arms around me to keep me anchored to him. Hux leans down and sucks my clit into his mouth and I fucking detonate.

My vision turns black as I scream out and come harder than I ever have in my life.

Hux pulls his fingers out and presses the pad of his tumb against my clit and opens his mouth making me squirt all over his face. Watching him swallow my release is... fucking sexy.

I have never known any guy to care enough about a woman coming. No, that's a lie. I did know a couple of guys but they are currently in this sauna with me. It's a fucking pity that the only three guys I have ever felt something for hate me for a lie I was forced to tell.

It's been two weeks of having Lennon here with us, each day we change up what we do with her. Some nights we make her put on a show while we film it before we fuck her, other nights we wear the masks and chase her ass down and fuck her hard. We have defiled every surface of this cabin with our cum. The whole house reeks of sex and I fucking love it. I only wear my mask on the nights we hunt her, so does Hux, but Dad never takes his off whenever she is around.

"I think something is wrong with Lennon." At Huxley's panicked tone I turn away from the window in the living room.

"What do you mean?" Dad asks from his seat at the dining table. The concerned look on Hux's face has me crossing the room to stand in front of him.

"Why do you think something is wrong with her?" I ask.

He shakes his head and frowns. "I went down to give her some lunch and she's laying in the corner of the cage shivering and groaning—" He doesn't get a chance to finish his sentence, Dad and I are both rushing past him and heading down to the basement. I come to a halt in front of her cell. Yes, we may be fucking her every night but that doesn't mean she gets to sleep upstairs with us. Dad enters the cell and crouches down beside her. "His mask," Hux whispers beside me.

My eyes widen when I realize he's right, Dad isn't wearing his mask but Lennon doesn't seem coherent enough to even notice. Dad scoops her up into his arms and stands.

"She has a fever," he states matter of factly and doesn't hang around. He just stalks out of the basement with Hux and me trailing after him. I say nothing as he passes the living room and heads down the hall to the bathroom. He gently places her on her feet then cups her face between his hands. Her eyes open but you can tell she can't focus on anything.

"My... head," she says, barely above a whisper. I flinch at the hint of pain in her tone. When she begins to sway, I dart forward but the bathroom is so fucking small that my dad blocks my path to her. Huxley is right behind me, I can feel his hot breath on the back of my neck.

"Get her some painkillers," Dad barks at Hux. When he disappears from the room he looks at me. "Help me strip her clothes off. She needs to get in the shower." I help Dad remove her clothes, cringing every time she groans or whimpers, her skin is hot to the touch but she's shivering like she's outside in the snow. "Turn the shower on warm." I do as he asks and step back. I watch him as he gently lifts her and climbs inside the stall with her plastered against his chest. His arms band around her waist, holding her upright. Hux enters and stands beside me with a glass of water and two white pills in the palm of his hand.

Neither of us have any idea what the fuck to do, Dad is the only person with any type of experience when it comes to sickness and caring for someone. I feel utterly fucking useless and I hate it.

Looking at her and seeing how vulnerable she is right now, knowing we are the reason she is in this state, kills me. We knew there was a high chance she would get sick after being out in the snow naked, but when she didn't get sick the next day we thought nothing of it.

"She was fine last night," Hux mutters.

I place my hand on his shoulder and squeeze reas-suringly. "It's not your fault." Guilt laces my own words and I know he won't find comfort from what I said, but I won't allow him to blame himself when we all had a hand in this happening.

"I... My... Sorry," she mumbles. She's so disoriented and weak. Dad is holding her weight completely and she hasn't stopped shivering.

"Why isn't she warm yet?" I snap.

Dad is grinding his teeth and trying to remain calm, this is the most tender he has been to her since we brought her here. His mouth says he hates her but the way he is holding her protectively tells a different story.

"Get some towels." I snag a couple towels, then hold one open for him to pass her to me. He gently turns and places her in my waiting arms, she falls into me as I wrap the towel around her quivering body. Hux comes forward and helps her take the pills. She coughs and struggles to swallow them down, but manages to do it. Hux and I have barely finished drying her when my dad steps out and strips his soaked clothes off. A groan escapes her before she passes out. I catch her with ease and lift her into my arms.

I stalk out of the bathroom and head down the hall to my bedroom with Hux on my heels. He draws the covers back on my bed for me. I gently lay her down and growl at the sight of her shivering. We tuck her in as best we can. Dad comes in with another blanket and places it on top of her for extra warmth, but her lips are still blue and the shivering hasn't lessened.

"Body heat," Hux mutters.

I turn to him and frown. "What?"

He rolls his eyes. "Body heat is the best thing. We need to strip down and climb in with her." I nod and begin stripping off with him. We both climb on either side of her. When my skin comes into contact with her I hiss.

"She's burning up," I state.

"We need the fever to break," Dad announces.

"How do we do that?" I ask.

He keeps his gaze on her as he answers me in a tight tone. "We can't, she has to do it on her own." I balk at him.

"There has to be something we can do!" I snap.

Dad shoots me a sympathetic look. "No. She has to do this on her own. We just have to try to help her through it and keep her fluids up so she doesn't get dehydrated." It's only then I notice he is standing there in nothing but a towel.

"Go change before you end up like her." My tone is firm and filled with anger but I can't find it within myself to care. It's wrong of me to place blame on him but I can't help it. When he leaves the room, Hux and I press in closer to her so she is sandwiched between the both of us. For the first time having her naked and pressed against me doesn't make my cock hard. Huxley snaps me out of my inner turmoil when he reaches over and cups my cheek, pulling my gaze to him.

"Are you ready to admit that this game of revenge is over?" he asks softly.

My brows bunch in confusion. "What are you saying?"

He smiles sadly. "I love you, Stone. Always have and always will, but I love her too and I know you feel the same way I do. She fucked up and cost us all something we can never get back. I think it's time we all stopped lying to ourselves and admit that Lennon St James is here because we want her to be, not because we want to hurt her."

I mull over his words for a long while and allow them to sink in. I look down at her and stare at her pale face. I was so hell bent on making her pay for taking my dad from me that I didn't realize I was falling in love with her all over again.

"She will never forgive us for what we have done to her," I whisper.

Hux smiles knowingly. "Baby, that girl has been in love with you and your dad since you both walked into her life. If it's forgiveness you're looking for, then get on your knees and pray for it because nothing you have done to her isn't something she didn't want."

Forgive me father for I give no fucks about passing those pearly gates as long as I get keep her.

Four days.

Four-fucking-days!

She has been in bed, unmoving, not eating and only managing to keep down the water we are forcing down her throat. The fever has yet to break. The three of us are taking turns laying with her and keeping her warm. Huxley and Stone have headed into town to grab some supplies, leaving me alone here with her. Having her in my arms feels so right yet wrong at the same time.

"Mom." I tense at the sound of her voice. She keeps mumbling incoherent things and we haven't been able to make sense of what she is saying for days.

"Shhhh," I coo as I gather her up and pull her against me, then run my fingers through her hair. She's still burning up and I just know that if this fever doesn't break soon we'll need to end this thing and take her to the hospital.

"Don't... make me lie..." I tense and close my eyes, biting back my anger, now is not the time for me to lose my shit over her sending me to prison. "Not Stone." My eyes snap open at the sound of my son's name. My breathing turns erratic as I wait for her to keep muttering but she's silent for so long I fear she won't speak again. "Kin..." My name sounds like a plea and the urge to comfort her and take away her pain is fierce. "He didn't touch me." The oxygen inside me evaporates.

I wait with bated breath for her to keep speaking. I'm hanging onto every word yet she remains tight lipped. I didn't realize how much I wanted to hear her reason why she lied about me until now. I want—no, I fucking need to know why she lied. The one night she came to me after her mother took off on another one of her benders, shit got out of hand. I knew she was sleeping with my son and that he and Hux loved her, but I never stopped her when she dropped to her knees in front of me and sucked my dick.

I wanted her so fucking badly but she was off limits. She was my stepdaughter, and me lusting after her was wrong. But then she turned eighteen and everything changed.

"Dad?" I shake my head to clear my thoughts and

look over to see Hux and Stone standing in the doorway with worry lines marring their faces. These boys are here because of me. I made them put their lives on hold for my revenge. I stole Lennon from her life at college and I had no fucking right to do that to any of them.

I close my eyes and exhale slowly before finally looking at my boys again. "Get her some clothes, we're taking her to the hospital." The shock on their faces is granted, for two days they have been begging me to take her to a doctor and I refused. I didn't want to admit it to myself but I was terrified of losing her. Once she woke up and was fine, I wouldn't be able to get to her again. The fear of never being able to touch her, hold her or kiss her has been what's holding me back, but that was selfish.

I'm done lying to myself.

Yes, I blamed her for robbing me of time with my son and ruining my life, but the real reason I was so angry with her was because she broke my heart and I didn't even see her betrayal coming.

Stone sat in the back seat with her while Hux rode shotgun beside me. The snow covering the roads made the drive slow but as we pulled up in front of the entrance of the hospital my real fear kicked in.

I know Lennon's friends would have reported her missing and the second we walk in there with her and they recognize who she is, cops will be swarming this place in minutes. Resigned to my fate, I put the car in park, then turn to look at both Hux and Stone.

"You two aren't coming in."

Both of their faces morph into anger. "Fuck you," Stone bites out.

"You can't stop us," Hux adds.

I reach over and grip the back of Huxley's neck and pull him in until our foreheads touch. "You're a good fucking man, Huxley Verlies, and I know you love my son, which is why I'm asking you to do the right thing here."

"What are you asking me, Kin?" he asks hesitantly.

I try to smile reassuringly but fail. "I'm going to take her in there and you are going to take Stone back—"

"I'm not fucking leaving you or her."

I ignore Stone's protest as I push on. "—to the cabin. When I take her in there and give her name, they will have cops here in minutes and I won't have either of you two going down for kidnapping a college girl when it was my idea."

Huxley's eyes widen in fear as he reels back and shakes his head. "Kin, I can't—"

"I've survived prison once, I will do it again, but I won't be able to live inside a cage again if I know the both of you are in there with me. I need you to do this for me." His mouth opens but no words come out. I turn to my son and smile. His eyes are filled with unshed tears and that shit fucking breaks me inside.

"Dad, I can't let you do this," he whispers.

"You can and you will. I got this, Son, but I need you to let her go when I step out of this car." He shakes his head, trying to deny what I'm saying so I push on. "Live your life, Stone. You and Hux deserve that. You have enough money to never work a day in your life and travel the world. Don't throw your life away like I did. Your grandfather's investments are still generating millions each year. You will be fine, Son."

I step out of the car without waiting for his response and move to the back to pull the door open. I lean in to gather Lennon in my arms but Stone won't let go. I shoot Hux a look, begging him for his help. With a defeated nod he reaches back and grips Stone's shoulder, drawing his focus to him.

"You have to let go. We will fight this and help him

however we can but we can't do that if we are all arrested."

"He's my dad." Stone fights back.

"And I always will be, Son. It's my job to look out for you so let me do that." I manage to pull her free of his hold and gather her in my arms. I look back at both of them and nod. "Get out of here and don't come back. I love you both." Hearing my son scream for me and begging me to not go will haunt me for the rest of my days, but I don't look back as I keep heading for the entrance. Once I enter I call for help. Nurses begin rushing toward me. Before they take her from me, I place a soft kiss on her lips. "I will search a hundred worlds for you and live a hundred lives just so I can find you in every life and love you, my little convict."

The past six weeks have been a whirlwind.

When I woke up in the hospital I was fucking terrified. I had no idea what had happened or how I had ended up there. I asked the nurses and doctors where Kincaid, Stone and Huxley were, but none of them would give me an answer. Police officers came in and questioned me, asking about my abduction. That shit threw me for a loop.

Turns out, Molly had reported me missing the next day after I didn't show up at the club and I love her for doing that but I can't help but be slightly bitter toward her for it as well. The second I was released, I went straight to the police station to set the story straight. I told them I wasn't kidnapped and that I just... took off for a while to clear my head and happened to bump into Kincaid who was caring for me and then took me to the hospital.

I know they don't believe me and I don't care, I won't allow that man to be sent away again because of me. I wasn't strong enough to speak my truth before, but I am not that same girl anymore. I will fight for him and make sure the fucking world knows he never hurt me. I spoke to detectives about what my mother had forced me to do and how she manipulated me to lie. I don't know if me telling the truth now will help and I know it won't erase what I put him through but the least I can do is clear his fucking name.

"Len?" I turn away from my laptop screen and look at Molly. She's sitting on my bed with a worried look on her face. Our relationship has been strained since I came back to school. I know she is giving up time with her guys to spend it with me and I appreciate her for worrying about me, but she doesn't need to.

"Yeah?"

"Don't bite my head off, okay?"

I sigh and nod. "Just ask me whatever it is you want to," I say dejectedly.

"I was there for you when Kincaid was sent to prison but you never told me why he was sent there."

Guilt churns inside me. "My mom manipulated me into lying to the cops. She found out I was sleeping with Stone and Huxley." Molly's eyes widen in surprise but I don't let that derail me. "Mom wanted to love Kincaid but she loved her drugs more. When they met she was clean for a year, but after they got married Kin's companies were thriving and he was away a lot, so she was lonely and depressed and turned to drugs. Her addiction got out of control. Kin and I got close as we cared for her and tried to get her help and somewhere along the way, I started looking at him differently."

"You fell in love with your stepdad?"

I nod. "Kin cut her off from all the accounts so she couldn't buy drugs. He sent her to rehab. When she got back, she hated him for trying to help and took off for a while. I was left with Hux, Stone and Kin and one night, I went downstairs and he was just there looking so fucking good I couldn't hold back anymore. I dropped to my knees and... well you can imagine what happened and because karma is a bitch, my mom chose that night of all nights to come home. She found me naked and on my knees with her husband's cock down my throat."

"What the fuck," she breathes out.

"Yeah. She kicked Kin out and because he's a good man he left without an argument. The next day she gave me an ultimatum. I either go to the cops and say Stone raped me or tell them it was Kincaid."

Molly gasps and reels back. "What the fuck!"

"Kincaid never touched me, *I* touched him." Tears prick the backs of my eyes. "I refused and she went nuts. She said she would tell them it was Stone. She thought if she blamed Stone, Kin would pay her whatever she wanted to keep his son from going to prison. I couldn't lie and blame Stone so she pushed me to say it was Kin. She thought all his assets would go to her but what she didn't know was Kin had everything in a trust and it would all go to Stone. She never got a single fucking penny."

When a lone tear rolls down my cheek, Molly leaps off the bed and rushes over to me to wrap me in a hug. "I'm so sorry, Len. I had no fucking idea."

"I was a fucking coward," I choke out.

Molly pushes me back and grips my shoulders while holding my gaze with a firm look on her face. "You didn't do anything wrong. Your mother manipulated you—"

"I tried to go back and tell them the truth but they told me it was victim guilt and that they wouldn't allow a rapist to go free."

"You were in love with him and as terrible as it sounds, he wouldn't hate you for choosing to save his son."

"Molly, I was eighteen. I knew better than to lie to the cops but I did it anyway, and I ruined their lives. I stayed silent for years because I was a fucking coward and let an innocent man rot in prison because I was too weak to stand up to my drug addict mother."

"Lennon, you aren't weak. You are the strongest person I know and you never give up."

"They're gone. I have no idea where they are. I thought after I told the cops what happened with Kincaid that they would release him and they would come find me again but..." I can't finish the sentence thanks to the giant lump in my throat.

"You are Lennon St James and you do not quit! If I had known you weren't in any danger, I swear I would never have reported you missing. I am so sorry, Len." I pull her to me and hug her tight.

"I love you for caring enough to do that for me," I say quietly.

"Let me help you find your guys."

I pull back and look at her. "How the hell are we going to find them if the police can't even locate them?" The detective I spoke with has been trying to locate Kincaid to bring him in for questioning and to let him know I recanted my statement. I have a court date set to appear for wrongfully accusing someone, but my lawyer says I should get off with a slap on the wrist given I was coerced into lying by my mother. Knowing that doesn't make me feel better though. She was a piece of shit and I should have known better than to lie.

My lie ruined not only their lives but mine as well

and now, I am left broken and in pieces because they are gone again and this time, it wasn't because they were forced to leave, it's because they wanted to.

"You do know that my boyfriends have really good connections, right?" she says smugly.

"And?" I press.

"Brayden knows a PI who is willing to help us find them if that's what you want?" My eyes widen in surprise.

"Seriously?" My tone is thick with emotion.

"Len, you're my best friend and I would do anything for you like you would me. Let me help you find your guys."

"Thank you," I force out past the lump in my throat.

"Say a little prayer, babe, because we might need some help from the man above."

I snort. "We are the last people he is going to help. You're fucking your stepbrothers and I've been fucking my stepdad, stepbrother and his best friend."

Molly cringes. "Yeah, maybe it's best to leave the big man out of this one."

Christmas came and went without any joy, we didn't have a tree. None of us celebrated the New Year. The three of us have been existing but not really living. None of us mentions her name. Ever since Kin was released we all made a pact to never look back and just move forward. We've been living in the cabin, out of all the nice houses they own we chose to remain here because it reminds us of her.

Stone and I have been burying ourselves in work. With Kin to keep distracted, we never got involved much with all the companies or the investments his grandfather made to form their wealth, but it's not like we have much to do to keep our minds occupied these days.

"We're leaving tomorrow," Kincaid announces,

drawing our attention to him. I cut a glance at Stone and raise a brow. He shrugs a shoulder.

"Why?" I ask.

Kin turns away from us and gazes out the window. "Because we can't keep living in the past. My name is cleared now. I hired the best lawyers to help *her* with her hearing and from what they tell me her case went well and she will serve no time. But, we can't keep living out here with the memories of her being here with us."

I remain silent while Stone sighs and nods. "You're right."

"Where are we going?" I ask.

Kin shrugs. "Anywhere but here. Finish what you're working on and then go pack. I hear the house in Aspen is nice this time of year, so we might go there." I don't say it because I know we are all thinking it, Aspen is a long fucking way from Lennon.

Stone and I finish our reports in silence. Once I'm done, I pack my laptop up, then head to my room to pack. It's not like we won't ever come back here some day, but I personally won't come back for a really long time. Stone doesn't even sleep in his bed anymore, he sleeps in my room every night because he says his bed smells like her.

Every night we lose ourselves in each other but neither of us want to admit that there is now a void between us and that void is a green-eyed, brown-haired beauty that is currently living her best life in college mere hours away from us... soon to be a plane fucking ride away from us.

I spend the rest of the evening packing my bags without any thought until I find my mask in one of my drawers. I stare down at it, remembering how amazing it felt to chase her ass down every night, knowing that she would submit to us and allow us to use her like a filthy whore and loved every minute of it.

"I'm beat," Stone says as he enters the room. I close the drawer and nod. He and I silently undress, then climb into bed. There was never this divide between us before and I begin to worry we will never be able to fill it, because there was only one person who could complete us.

"Do you think she ever thinks about us?" His question stumps me for a second.

"Yeah, I do."

"Do you think we're wrong for staying away?"

I exhale slowly before answering. "We drugged her, chained her up, fucked her like savages and then she nearly died because of us. I think it's the least we can do is stay away, even if it fucking hurts."

Stone is silent for a long while and I begin to think he's fallen asleep until he speaks. "I love her, Hux."

"I know."

"Does it bother you?" His tone is tinged with worry and I can't help but smile.

"Does it bother you that I love her too?"

He chuckles. "They say you never forget your first and she was yours."

I elbow the fucker in the ribs. "You were hers."

"Yeah, but I also knew she loved you and my dad even back then, and it never bothered me. I was fucking happy because that meant I didn't have to give her up for you or you for her and sharing her with my dad never bothered me either." I open my mouth to answer but then snap it closed when the lights shut off.

"Fuck, must be a fuse," I say as I climb out of the bed. Stone follows my lead. As I open the door I spot Kin across the hall with his phone light on.

"Power must have tripped," he says.

"Yeah, let me get a shirt then I'll come help—" Before I can finish speaking, the sound of something dragging along the wooden floor near the living room draws our attention. Kin shuts off his light and the second he does a strange pink light can be faintly seen. The three of us quietly make our way toward the living room, ready to beat the shit out of whoever the fuck thought it would be a good idea to try break in and rob us, but the instant we all enter the living room we freeze.

"The fuck," I breathe out at the sight in front of us.

A woman wearing a mask like ours but with pink LED lights stands there with... it's hard to make out in the dark but it looks like a fucking machette. She's wearing a black hoodie and dark pants but that's about all I can make out in this lighting.

"Who the fuck are you?" Stone snaps.

"Tick Tock, little convict," she says in a robotic tone, then swings the machete up to rest on her shoulder.

"Lennon?" Kin breathes out, causing me to gasp.

She strikes out and points the machete right at Kin's chest. "*Say that fucking name again and I'll rip your tongue out and fuck you with it.*" I choke on my laugh, that was the same fucking thing he said to her when she said his name.

I raise my hands and take a step forward but stop when she presses the blade into my chest. "Okay, little convict. I'll play your game, baby. What do you want from us?"

"Your fear. Your mind. Your body," she answers in that fucking robotic tone. I get why she hated it when we used the masks now.

"Is that all?" Stone presses as he moves to stand beside me. "Because we want more than that from you, convict."

I feel the blade start to tremble against my chest but don't call her on it.

"We want your submission," Kin says as he comes to stand on my other side. "Your body. But, most of all, we want a fucking place in your heart." The machete drops from her hand and clangs against the wooden floor. The silence is so fucking loud you could hear a pin drop.

I can tell she is floundering from the revelation so I choose to help her out. "You get to call the shots tonight, convict. What do you want us to do?"

She squares her shoulders and runs her gaze over all of us. The three of us are standing here in nothing but our briefs. "Run."

They waste no time.

The three of them turn and race for the back door. I know why they chose to run outside practically naked. They want to even the odds because that's what I did for them. I chase after them with a smile on my face. I don't know what I was thinking but I never expected the three of them to split off and go in different directions. I growl in frustration and bank left to chase Stone into the woods. How the fuck can he see so well in the dark? Even with the light of my mask I'm struggling. When I lose sight of them, I slow to a stop and spin around in a circle and strain my hearing to listen for the sound of snow crunching beneath his feet.

"Imagine losing your prey?" I spin around to the right at the sound of Huxley's voice. I squint my eyes, trying to spot him but come up empty.

"It's clear we're the hunters." I turn to the right at the sound of Kin's voice but I see nothing.

A shriek tears out of me when an arm wraps around my waist from behind and I feel someone pressed against my back. "You will always be our prey, little convict," Stone purrs in my ear, making me moan and melt into him. He grips my throat with his free hand and tilts my head back so I'm forced to look up at him. "You had a chance at freedom from us, baby."

"I don't want it," I admit.

I loll my head to the side at the sound of the other two approaching us—fuck they look hot. Hux's brown hair is a mess but it's the hungry look in his brown eyes that has me clenching my thighs. I look at Kincaid next and a lump forms in my throat at the sight of him. His salt and pepper hair is slicked back and his glorious body is on display for me to drink in every inch of him.

"The mask is hot and everything, babe, but for what we have in store for you, we're gonna need that mouth to be free." Huxley's dark promise sends a shiver of need down my spine. Kin steps forward and tears the mask off. The second we lock eyes the world fucking shifts. No longer are there any boundaries between us, this is real and we're forced to face each other.

When Kincaid leans down and smashes his lips against mine, my mind blanks. I'm burning with need for them. I don't realize he has lifted me off the ground until he begins walking. My legs and arms are wrapped around him in a bruising hold but he doesn't seem to care as he fucks my mouth with his tongue.

The taste of him is sweeter than honey.

I don't realize we're inside the cabin until I hear the door slam closed. I break the kiss and look back at Stone. "Where's Hux?" I ask breathlessly as Kin carries me into the living room.

"Fixing the power." I chuckle but it dies the second Kincaid throws me onto the bed. I bounce once before he is on top of me, pinning me in place with his weight.

The light in the hallway flicks on, offering me enough light to see the lust in Kin's eyes but I also see… love. I reach up and cup his cheek in my hand and stare into his eyes.

"I'm so sorry," I whisper.

He shakes his head. "I know why you did it and I don't blame you. It would have killed me to lose my son. You made the right choice, Lennon." I don't realize I'm crying until he swipes my tears away with his thumbs.

"Little convict, as touching as this moment is and everything, my cock is begging to be inside you and it's been denied the warmth of your cunt for too long." Stone's crass words snap me out of it and heat surges inside me. Huxley enters the room and suddenly the space feels too small. My clothes feel so tight and restricting, my panties are fucking ruined. I'm so wet and my pussy is pulsing with need.

"I need to feel you all inside me," I moan as I try to grind against Kincaid, but the bastard lifts his hips off me, denying me the friction I'm craving. I whimper in protest which causes him to smirk down at me smugly. I want to claw his face, I'm too turned on to be denied what I want right now.

"Tell us how bad you want to feel our cocks inside you," Hux growls.

"So fucking bad, I'm so wet for you," I admit as I wrap my arms around Kin's neck and try to pull him down to me, but he doesn't budge an inch. I flop back against the bed and groan in frustration.

"You may have come back and thought you were the boss, little convict, but make no fucking mistake, we are the ones always in control," Stone vows as he climbs onto the bed beside us. I tilt my head back to look up at him and gasp at the sight of him kneeling by my head with his cock in his hand. I dart my tongue out to moisten my lips, my mouth is watering for a taste of him.

Kin slides off me and stands beside Hux. In unison they both push their briefs down, exposing their hard cocks. Hux lifts his hand and tosses a tube of lube to Kincaid. I watch with rapt attention as he squirts some onto his dick, then onto his palm and begins to stroke himself. He keeps his eyes on me the whole time until Stone and Hux begin tearing my clothes off. Hux brings my soaking wet panties to his nose and inhales, then groans.

"Fuck, she smells so sweet," he grits out, then rubs my panties on his cock, making me gasp at the sight.

"Hux, get the fuck on the bed and make that slut ride you." I moan at Kin's crass words. Hux moves to obey his command and lays in the middle of the bed. I shift to accommodate his size and waste no time straddling his lap. Huxley grips my waist, the feeling of his hands on me again after so long is fucking perfect, his hands burn into my skin and I relish the feeling.

"I got you, little convict," Stone says as he reaches between me and Hux and grips his cock, making the man beneath me groan. I shiver in anticipation as he lines him up with my entrance. I gasp when I feel the head of his cock pushing inside me. Stone releases him and grips my throat, forcing my focus on him. "I want to look at you as your greedy little cunt swallows every inch of him." A moan slips free without consent. I slowly lower onto Hux, dragging it out just to please Stone.

"Fuck, she's so damn tight," Huxley pants as I slam down onto him. I cry out, only to be silenced when Stone claims my mouth, swallowing my cries.

"Hold her ass open for me," I hear Kin say as the bed dips with his weight. Huxley grips the globes of my ass and I moan, breaking the kiss with Stone so I can lean forward. I plant my arms on either side of Hux's head and shiver when I feel the cold lube hit my ass. Kincaid swirls his finger around my hole and makes me lurch forward when he presses a finger inside me.

"Fuck! Her pussy is choking my dick so fucking good right now," Hux growls. Stone moves to the top of the bed and straddles Huxley's head. I open my mouth ready to taste him but pause when he groans in pleasure. I look down to see Hux's face buried in his ass.

That is so fucking hot!

Kin continues to stretch me out while I lean forward and suck Stone into my mouth, whimpering at the taste of him. I swirl my tongue around his length and love the way he shivers. I'm unable to stop myself from grinding down on Hux, I'm so needy and ready for them to devour me and every fucking inch of my body. I want them to ingrain themselves inside me, tattoo me from the inside and brand me as theirs forever.

TWENTY-ONE

STONE

The feeling of both their mouths on me is fucking everything.

Hux is tongue fucking my ass so good I'm trembling, mix that with the feeling of her bobbing up and down on my dick, it is almost enough for me to pass the fuck out from how good it feels. When she gasps and tenses, I look down to see my dad pushing inside her ass. He places his hands on top of Hux's and I can tell my man loves that my dad is touching him because he quakes beneath us.

Huxley has always had a crush on my dad and I think secretly that my dad likes him too, but is too proud to admit it. One day soon, he will give in though and my boy will finally be able to have my dad's dick inside him while I watch.

"Hmmmm," Lennon cries out around me when

Dad slams inside her. Huxley pushes his tongue deeper inside me and I grunt my approval.

"Look at this filthy little slut. Taking all our cocks like she was fucking made to," Dad says. Lennon shivers and pushes back against him, demanding more which just earns her a slap to the ass that has her lurching forward and choking on my dick. "You get what the fuck we give, nothing more, you desperate slut."

I thrust forward, making her gag harder and loving the sound, I tangle my fingers in her hair and keep her in place as I push inside her deeper, forcing her to take every fucking inch. She taps on my thigh, making me pull back. She releases me with a wet pop. She sits up and rests her back against Dad. I narrow my eyes at the bitch, until she grips my dick in her hand and begins to stroke me.

"I want you to watch your dad and boyfriend fuck me. I want you to hear every fucking sound I make as they make me come." Hux releases her ass and cups my balls in one hand then uses the other to wrap around my leg to hold me in place. A loud moan tumbles out of me at the feeling. Dad cups her tits and slams inside her, making her cry out.

"Tell my son how good I feel inside you." His request has my brows raising and my dick twitching in her hand.

"So good, he fills me so well but, having Huxley inside my pussy at the same time is everything."

"His cock is mine, you little whore, remember that," I grit out as I fight off my impending orgasm.

"Fuck!" she cries out when she slams down onto Hux. "Yes, keep fucking me just like that," she screams. She drops her grip on me to place her hands on Hux's chest as they both fuck her hard and deep, forcing her over that fucking cliff so she can free fall into ecstasy. "Stone!" she screams my name as she comes. In a bold move she lifts off Hux, then rubs her clit and squirts all over me and Hux's stomach. I jerk back and shift to the side, then down and lick her pussy, moaning at the taste of her cum. Her fingers tangle in my hair, holding me in place as she grinds against my face. "Holy shit, Kin, keep fucking me. I'm gonna come on his face."

Dad increases his tempo, slamming into her ruthlessly as I suck her clit into my mouth. "I'm gonna come," Dad roars.

"Come with me!" Lennon cries out. Three more thrusts and both of them are crying out and shuddering as they come. Her release fills my mouth and I swallow every drop of it, loving the taste of her—she tastes like fucking honey. Dad eases out of her and climbs off the bed. I claim his position. Hux lines himself up and slams inside her, making her scream. I push inside her with ease, my dad's release mixed with the lube makes it easy to slip in.

"Fuck, let me record this," Dad says, then grabs his phone and begins recording us.

"I want to hear you come, baby," I say to Hux.

"Make me. Fuck her so hard her pussy milks me of every last drop like a good little whore." I rise to the challenge and fuck her with every ounce of strength I have, forcing them both to take and feel every damn inch of me. The sounds coming from Lennon are like music to my fucking ears.

"I'm gonna come!" the greedy bitch calls out. I reach around and grip her throat, applying enough pressure to restrict her airways and heighten her release. She gasps and grips my forearm, but I don't release my hold. When her orgasm slams into her, it sets off mine and Hux's making us all come in unison. The three of us are panting, sweating and a mess of limbs but nothing has ever felt more perfect.

I gently ease out of her and collapse beside them. She's flopped forward onto Hux and lays on top of him panting with her eyes closed. She looks utterly spent and so well fucked. I smirk when Dad comes to lay on the other side of the bed and reaches out to run his fingers through her hair, making her fucking purr and smile sleepily.

We lay like this, just touching and soaking in the

moment. After what happened, I never thought we would ever get a chance to be together again. I am so grateful to have been proven wrong. Lennon St James belongs right here, with us.

"We're leaving tomorrow," Dad says, breaking the silence. Lennon's eyes snap open and I see the heartache reflected in those green orbs.

"Oh," is all she manages to say. That one word is filled with so much anguish and pain.

"We're going to Aspen," I add.

She tries to smile happily but the unshed tears in her eyes give away the pain she is in. "That's... good," she forces out, then sits up. She plasters a fake smile on her face as she climbs off Hux and slips off the bed. She looks around for her clothes on the floor and when she finds them, I glare at her as she starts to get dressed.

"The fuck are you doing?" Hux bites out as he sits up, scowling at her.

She pulls her shirt on, then tugs on her jeans before facing us. "I think it would be good if I left now, to beat the traffic—"

"It's two in the fucking morning," Dad snarls.

She cringes then shrugs. "I have an early class in the morning?"

"You asking or telling us, little convict?" I throw back.

She sighs and her shoulders droop. "Look, let's not make this a big thing. I came back, you guys are leaving, and now I need to learn to live my life again. I love you all and I will never not love you, but I won't hold you guys back. I stole enough time from you all and I won't take any more." When she turns away from us to grab her hoodie and shoes, I start to panic and jump to my feet. Hux and Dad do the same, which causes her to turn back to us.

"Where the fuck do you think you are going?" Dad snaps.

She frowns and reels back shocked by his outburst. "Home?"

Hux steps forward. "You are home," he says in a firm tone.

"No, you're going to Aspen to start a new life." The tinge of anger in her tone has me smiling, which earns me a glare from her.

"Yes, *we* are," Dad confirms.

She rolls her eyes. "Good. Go enjoy your life," she snaps, then attempts to walk out, but I grip her arm and yank her back, forcing her to face me.

"When he says we, he means *we* as in him, Hux, me and... *you*."

Her mouth pops open. "We're all in love with you, little convict. We tried to give you a life without us, which is why we were leaving in the morning to head to Aspen, but then you came and found us." At Dad's words, tears begin to roll down her cheeks.

"We don't want a life without you," Hux adds.

"You are the glue to our family. If you don't want this, want us, then say it now or we're never going to let you go. I would hate to have to drug you and chain your sexy ass up again until you realize you love us too much to walk away."

Taking college classes online and moving to Aspen was not something I had planned on, but here we fucking are!

We're about to celebrate our first Christmas here and as part of my gifts from my guys they flew Molly, Brayden, Kingston and Justin out here to spend the holidays with us. Our house is huge and has more bedrooms than we know what to do with. Hux keeps hinting that we need to fill the vacant seven bedrooms with children and to my utter shock, Kincaid is on board with the idea. Stone is the only one who is on my side and agrees to wait until I finish college before thinking about kids.

He and Hux have even signed up to take classes online and I am so fucking proud of them.

"That is the sexiest sight I have ever seen," Molly

says, pulling me from my thoughts. I follow her line of sight to look out on the back patio to see the six guys, all shirtless and sitting in the hot tub. The sight of my guys has my pussy pulsing with need. My hunger for them hasn't lessened one little bit.

"God, they look like sex on fucking legs," I agree.

"So…" I turn to Molly and frown at the anxious look on her face.

"You okay?" I press. She nibbles on her bottom lip and nods, but I can tell a question is burning inside her. "Spit it out!"

"Any chance you guys are into voyeurism?" I choke on my spit.

"Come again?" I squeak out.

She turns a bright shade of red and shrugs her shoulders. "It was just a thought."

"Lay it out for me, Lollie."

"You get to watch us and we get to watch you guys, no touching of the others just our own guys." I look back at the six of them sitting in the tub and grin.

"You keep your hands off my guys and I'll do the same. Your guys can't touch me and mine can't touch you?"

She smiles wide and nods excitedly. "Deal." I tip back my glass of bourbon, then yank my shirt over my head. I can feel my guys staring at me. I face them with a sinister smirk. I spot Molly's guys watching her with a hungry look as the both of us put on a little strip tease. Not once do any of the guys peak where they shouldn't, they only have eyes for their own girl and I fucking love that.

Molly interlocks her fingers with mine and leads me through the back door toward the hot tub, where all the guys sit wearing hungry looks.

"We're about to try something and as much as you are going to hate it, Molly and I are calling the shots," I announce.

"Baby, you call whatever the fuck you want as long as you bring that pussy over here and sit on my face." I shoot Hux a wink and step into the tub with Molly at my side.

Forgivness is for fucking pussies. I don't want the Father above to fogrive me for shit because I have no damn regrets, and will continue to sin every-fucking-day if it means I get to keep getting my brains fucked out by my guys.

THANK YOU!

Are you enjoying your banishment from the man
above?

Thank you so much for reading Dirty Little Convict!
To say I loved this book is an understatement!
Each of these characters was a fucking dream to write
and damn did I have some fucking fun with certain
scenes. Turns out, I'm a dirty bitch at heart and have a
thing for daddy kinks.

I cannot thank you enough for reading *Dirty Little
Convict*, it means the world to me that you have taken a
chance on reading one of my books!

STALKER LINKS

Newsletter 🤍
Facebook 🤍
Reader's Group 🤍
Instagram 🤍
TikTok 🤍
Amazon 🤍
Website 🤍
Bookbub 🤍
Goodreads 🤍
Linktree 🤍

ACKNOWLEDGMENTS

Baby daddy, my main man, my bestie, you are the inspiration behind this dark book because I have envisioned doing all of the things the guys did to Len so many times to you. I would love to chain your ass up and lock you in a cage so you would be at my mercy and forced to endure all my sexual favors. Let's make that dream a reality, huh?

My demon spawn, you drive me crazy, have me pulling out my hair daily but fuck me, you both are everything and more to me. You both are my miracles and I will be forever grateful that you chose me to be your mum!

Leah, dear lord woman, I adore you beyond words! I am so grateful for you and all your support over the years, babe. I couldn't do this shit without you by my side.

Sarah, the best motherfucking PA that gets fired every other day because I have a meltdown. I don't deserve you, we know this, but I don't give a fuck because I'll never give you up and if you try to leave, I'll find you!

Lizz, I am running out of ways to express how much you mean to me and how grateful I am for you being here and taking a chance on little old me. You put up with my fucked-up schedule and never moan about me sending you book after book. You are the best fucking editor out there my friend.

My alpha's, Debbie, Clare, Erin and Samantha (number 2), Patti, Morgan, thank you all for being here and joining me on this fucked-up ride of smut and sinning. These books become what they are because of you all and for that I will be forever indebted to you.

My beta babes, Amber, Amanda, Nicole, Alex, Kira & Rizzo, saying thank you will never be enough. The amount of love and work you all put into these books means the world to me. I could never have asked for a better beta team.

My ARC army girls. You ladies are the best hype team in the world and I am truly thankful for all of you being here and coming along on this fucked-up ride as I try out new things and pump these books out.

My darling dark delicious readers, your support over the years means more than you will ever know. Without all of you I wouldn't be able to live out my dream of bringing these characters to life. Thank you!

Sam xxx

Also By Samantha Barrett

Mafia Romance's

https://books.bookfunnel.com/mafiaseries

Secret Society/ Bully/ Masked Men

https://books.bookfunnel.com/dirtytemptation

Sinners Welcome (Pure Smut Novellas)

https://books.bookfunnel.com/sinnerswelcome

Samantha's Entire Backlist

https://books.bookfunnel.com/SamanthasBookverse

ABOUT THE AUTHOR

Samantha Barrett is originally from Auckland, New Zealand but living in Brisbane, Australia.

Sam writes all things dirty dark and delicious with a side of twisted mind fuck.

She is a lover of all things red flags and an anti-hero is a must.

www.ingramcontent.com/pod-product-compliance
Lightning Source LLC
Chambersburg PA
CBHW061925220726
48287CB00018B/980